YOUR FREE BOOKS ARE WAITING

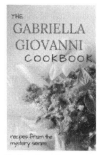
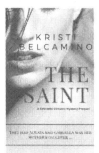
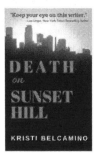

The CIA Dossier on Gabriella Giovanni

Recipes from the Gabriella Giovanni mystery Series

This novella is a prequel to the Gabriella Giovanni Mystery series

The first novella in the Tommy St. James mystery series

"Keep your eye on this writer."
—Lisa Unger, New York Times bestselling author

Sign up for Kristi Belcamino's no spam newsletter and get all these books for FREE.
Details can be found at the end of
BLESSED ARE THE PEACEMAKERS.

D1713179

Blessed are the Peacemakers

A GABRIELLA GIOVANNI MYSTERY

By Kristi Belcamino

Colleen,

I'm so lucky
to have you for
my mother-in-law'.
I love you!

x _Kusti B._

A sleek head encased in black rubber surfaced from the murky lake. The diver raised a gloved hand out of the water.

Another body.

Twelve bodies were already lined up on the beach, each encased in thick plastic that was not quite opaque enough to cloak their contents—bloated bodies and bulbous heads dotted with black holes where the eyes, mouth, and nose had once been. It was impossible to tell if the lumpy shapes were male or female.

The tipster who had called Gabriella Giovanni at her desk at the *Bay Herald* was right: Lake Josephine was a watery graveyard.

Gabriella had called the park police as soon as she began driving to the lake. Her call had paid off with a front row seat to the gruesome recovery effort. Sheriff's officials studiously ignored her, but made damn sure all the other reporters remained far behind the crime scene tape cordoning off the beach, a small playground and a parking lot. The rest of the lakeshore was dotted with small docks that led to private homes. A TV news crew halfway across the lake was interviewing someone on the dock of his lakeside home.

This stretch of the lake, a public park, was scattered with forgotten remnants from a day at the beach—a yellow shovel, dirty sock, broken bucket, pink sippy cup. One of the deputies had kicked the items into a small pile to make room for the bodies.

Gabriella knew this popular swimming spot would normally be packed on a sweltering day like today. But police tape blocked the main road from visitors. Many families, like the foursome that arrived with beach towels, probably walked to the lakeside park from a nearby housing development. The family stopped at the crime scene tape cordoning off the entrance to the parking lot and stared. The woman, holding a little girl's hand, stiffened as she caught sight of the rows of plastic-encased bodies on the beach.

Gabriella could stomach a lot. She'd seen her fair share of dead bodies—fresh ones at crime scenes and cold ones on steel slabs at the morgue. But the decomposing soggy messes encased in clear plastic bags were an entirely different story. As one diver flopped the new body on the sand, something on his wet suit got stuck on the plastic and it tore. Instantly, a brownish green foul mess seeped out onto the sand along with a smell that sent the diver keeling over, ripping at his mask so he could vomit.

The light breeze carried a whiff over to Gabriella. But unlike the decomposition smell that permeates a sanitary morgue, this scent was mixed with all sorts of horrors that had been festering under the plastic for God knows how long.

It was only the tiniest hint of scent, but it filled up her mouth and made Gabriella gag. She closed her eyes for a second, trying to regain her composure.

Several men in slacks and dress shirts huddled near the parking lot. One man, in sunglasses and a dark three-piece suit, kept shooting glances her way. She narrowed her eyes at him. Either he wanted to kick her out of the crime scene or he was waiting for her to realize she couldn't handle it and leave on her own.

If you think I'm going to puke or scream just because I'm a woman, you're wrong buddy.

She shot another glance at him. Not a cop. He was too refined. Too well-dressed. Too polished. Probably FBI. Only uptight government officials wore suits like that on an 80-degree day in California.

In a few minutes, the officials would give an official statement and then Gabriella could head back to the *Bay Herald* newsroom, and write up her story.

"*Stai bene?*" Are you okay?

It was the man in the dark suit. He stood right in front of the sun, which made his face a black mass without features. She squinted as he shifted and the sun struck her full in the eyes.

Although she looked stereotypically Italian—long dark hair, naturally full red lips, and ample curves—Gabriella was irritated. She was proud of her heritage, but something about this man automatically assuming she spoke Italian rubbed her wrong.

"I'm fine." There was not an ounce of warmth to her voice. She'd learned years ago as a cub reporter that most men wouldn't treat her like an equal unless she adopted their gruff seriousness.

A cloud went over the sun and Gabriella was able to see the man's face. A long scar ran across one sculpted cheekbone and curved toward his mouth.

Gabriella ignored the man with the Italian accent and took off toward the group of reporters starting to form around a man in gray suit. She ducked under the crime scene tape and stood behind the TV cameras on tripods, balancing on one foot at a time while she dumped sand out of her sandals.

A slim man with a ruddy complexion and bushy eyebrows that matched the longish silver hair brushed back away from his forehead, adjusted his tie and cleared his throat. Gabriella rummaged in her bag and got her pen and notebook ready.

"I'm Lucrèce Winoc, from the state public safety department's Division of Homeland Security and Emergency Management," the man said.

Gabriella's pen froze on the paper. She'd expected the sheriff or maybe even FBI.

"Good afternoon and thank you for coming." He didn't smile. "In a minute, I'll make a statement giving you what little information we have this early in the investigation. There are a lot of questions that remain unanswered, but we will tell you what we know that will not compromise this case. This is a very large operation, as you might have guessed, and we will not have many answers for you for some time."

Winoc shuffled some papers, but began without glancing at them.

"At nine this morning, our office received word that a body had been found in Lake Josephine and that there might be more than just the one."

A TV reporter leaned forward. "Is it true that a tipster called a newspaper reporter and that's how you learned about the bodies?"

Gabriella narrowed her eyes. This guy, who looked like an underwear model you'd see in tighty whiteys on a New York City billboard, was somehow plugged in. Hmmm. She'd better keep her eye on him.

"I'm not at liberty to say," Winoc said. "But I can tell you that the Ramsey County Sheriff's Office dive team has since recovered thirteen bodies."

A reporter with red spiral curls gasped. Gabriella wanted to roll her eyes. Run along to your stories about celebrity scandals and leave the big kids to their work here please.

"We are not done with our recovery efforts yet so we won't have a final count until probably sometime tomorrow. The divers will continue searching the lake through the night using spotlights that the Lake Josephine park police are providing."

"Can you tell us how many divers are out here?" another reporter asked.

Winoc glanced at a sheriff's deputy nearby.

"Eight on each team," the man said.

Winoc looked down at his sheet now and began to read. "This is an unspeakably horrific crime. We have lots of questions and very few answers, but rest assured, working together with the cooperation of the Ramsey County Sheriff's office and the Ramsey County Medical Examiner's unit, we will get to the bottom of this. We are going to be doing everything in our power to identify these tragic victims and make sure the perpetrators are brought to justice. Thank you. Any questions?"

"Mob?" one reporter asked. That's what Gabriella was going to ask, thinking of the man with the Italian accent. She glanced behind her. He was still on the beach, huddled with some other officials over one of the bodies. She watched him prod something on the sand with the toe of his expensive looking leather shoes. He glanced her way and she quickly turned back around. Something about the man made her uneasy.

"At this point," Winoc continued. "This early in the investigation, we have no way of knowing who is behind this."

The reporter with the good hair leaned over and whispered in Gabriella's ear. "Cartel."

So, that's why Homeland Security was involved.

He drew back with a knowing look. Gabriella leaned over and pressed her lips nearly against his ear, her voice softer than a whisper. "Just who *are* you banging anyway? The head of the CIA?" She pulled back and raised an eyebrow, waiting.

The woman with the red ringlets scowled.

The boy gave an impish shrug. "I have my ways."

She scribbled her cell phone number on the back of her card and handed it to him. "We should talk."

"Over dinner?" He smiled.

"How about this: I'll buy you a hot chocolate for your troubles," Gabriella said. "I'm sure Little Bo Beep over there would be happy to have dinner with you."

Stuffing her notebook in her bag, Gabriella turned to leave. He touched her arm, stopping her.

"Then I'm sure you have a lot to teach me."

She walked away without answering.

As the TV reporters rushed to edit footage in their big white vans, Gabriella huddled under a tiny tree that offered a bit of shade and dialed her husband, Agent Sean Donovan. The scent of Jasmine drifted by, a welcome relief from the putrid smell down by the beach. Gabriella leaned back against the rough bark of the tree, suddenly tired after standing for the past three hours.

Gabriella spoke before Donovan said hello: "Cartel."

"I know. I'm at the airport. I'm heading out. Your mom's home with Grace."

Gabriella's heart clenched a little. She wished Donovan had never taken that job with the DEA last year. At least when he was a detective he'd been able to come home most nights.

"I don't even get to kiss you goodbye?"

Donovan laughed. "You can make up for it next week when we're in Jamaica."

"God, I can't wait. When's the last time we took a vacation. Away from Grace that is?"

"That'd be never, Ella. That's why there'll be lots of kissing."

This time she laughed, as well. But quickly sobered. "I already miss you. How long will you be gone this time?"

"I told them I needed to be back by Saturday. I said I had important plans with my wife."

"You've said that before and they haven't listened."

"This time I'm dead serious and they know it. Nothing will stop me from my vacation alone with my wife. I'll be home in time. I promise. I'll be there."

"You better be, Donovan."

She clicked off and stared into the distance, not seeing anything.

Two months later ...

Gabriella squinted at the long bar of sunlight that somehow had seeped through her blinds to shine directly in her eyes. She reached behind her and chucked her pillow, sending the blinds clattering back into place, turning the room blissfully black again. Throwing the pillow had kicked up the unwashed scent that permeated her bedroom now. Half asleep, she lay back down on the bed sheets. She buried her face in the other pillow on the bed next to her and in a near dream state, repeated her unconscious ritual, the search for a familiar scent that had dissipated long ago. Instead, it smelled like her dirty greasy hair. As the fog lifted, it came to her—what she was trying so desperately to smell—any lingering remains of her husband's scent.

Staring into the blackness, her fuzzy mind instantly cleared. A sob escaped her mouth as the cobwebs cleared and the harsh reality of her life returned.

Donovan was dead.

Every day it was the same thing. She woke in a haze created by the remnants of sleeping pills wearing off. And then she remembered. And the pain was like a blow that made it hard to breathe, hard to see, and hard to move.

The red flashing numbers on the clock told her that even if she were to fall back to sleep, she'd have to get up soon to get Grace ready for school. Might as well do it now.

She swung her legs over the side of the bed and stood, straightening out her white nightgown with her palms. She had to get ready for another day of pretending to be alive. For Grace.

That's when she heard the little knock on her bedroom door, barely a tap, and an even smaller voice. "Mama?"

Closing her eyes, she swallowed back a sob before answering. She knew that Grace had been sitting outside her bedroom door for up to an hour, waiting for any sounds from inside.

"I'm awake, honey. I just have to use the bathroom and I'll be right out." Her attempt at chipper still sounded brittle and saccharine, but would have to do.

Gabriella waited until she heard the slow plodding footsteps of her seven-year-old daughter retreat into the other room before she headed into the master bathroom. Flicking on the light, she stared at her gaunt, gray face in the mirror. Sleeping pills and booze every night did not make for a vibrant complexion. It didn't matter. None of it mattered. She was doing everything she could do simply to get through her days. If she needed a tiny nudge in the form of a chemical and cocktail mix to make it through those last few hours of the day before she sunk into blessed oblivion, then so be it. At least she had managed not to down the whole prescription bottle at once. That was something.

Keeping it together all day long was as much as she'd been able to manage the past two months. If she didn't hold her shit, how could she expect Grace to survive?

For the seemingly millionth time, Gabriella felt a wave of admiration for her mother. Maria Giovanni had lost her young daughter and husband in one fell swoop so many years ago. Gabriella prayed every day she'd have the strength and grace her mother had shown for the past thirty years.

Splashing cold water on her face and then drying it off slowly, Gabriella stared at her own eyes in the mirror. Where was that strength? It was in her blood. Giovanni's were survivors. She needed it now more than ever. Pulling on her robe, she headed out to the rest of the penthouse.

CHAPTER THREE

Gabriella plopped a frozen waffle, syrup, and a glass of orange juice down on the breakfast table in front of Grace.

Her daughter pushed the plate away with a grimace. The kid was a gourmand at age seven. It wasn't her fault. Ever since she could put her thumb and forefinger together, she'd been eating San Francisco sourdough bread toasted and spread with local cheese and fresh preserves for breakfast. Or else homemade cardamom scones. Or Donovan's French toast. But no more.

Now it was all Gabriella could do to stick some frozen rectangles in the toaster and remember to cart the syrup to the breakfast table. At this point, she was even considering buying fruit cocktail in bulk to serve for meals.

"Eat your breakfast," she said, trying to hide the irritation in her voice. The kid was spoiled. When Gabriella was growing up, she and her two brothers fixed their own Pop Tart breakfasts. With a prickle of guilt, she remembered that's because when Gabriella's sister died, her mother hung up her apron and told them making breakfast was now their job. If they hadn't made their own food, they knew they

wouldn't see any until they got to school and had lunch in the cafeteria.

"Mama, can I read *The Hunger Games*." Grace was subtly

pushing her plate away from her, millimeter by millimeter.

"No way." Gabriella pushed the plate back in front of her.

"Why not?"

"You're seven-years-old."

"That counselor said I read at the level of a tenth grader."

"That doesn't matter."

"Come on! Tracy's mom let her read it."

"Then no for sure." Gabriella said lightly and leaned over to

pour syrup on her daughter's partly burned waffle. A tiny drop of syrup

dripped onto the table. Gabriella eyed the linen napkin by her plate but

decided she didn't feel like wiping up the spill.

Grace kept her eyes on her mother as she dipped her finger into

the mess, sucking the sweet syrup off, waiting for a scolding about

table manners that never came.

"Mama? Are you listening?"

Gabriella looked up confused. Had Grace been talking?

"I asked if Nana was coming over after school today?"

"I think so."

Grace shot her mother a frustrated look. Gabriella took a gulp of her coffee. She had to get it together. She was spacing out more often lately.

Her grief had turned to numbness. She didn't cry anymore. At least not weeping that brought any tears. She'd cried herself out the first month.

"Can I have milk instead of juice?"

Gabriella stood and headed toward the kitchen. The only thing keeping her in motion was going through the paces. At least the kid was eating her waffle. Nibbling at it, but at least taking a few bites. At first, when Donovan died, Grace refused to eat. That stopped when her therapist took her on a tour of the hospital and showed what happened to kid's who didn't eat. One glimpse of a girl with a feeding tube stuck down her nose did the trick. It was harsh, but then again, Grace's therapist didn't mess around when it came to kids withering away.

Gabriella plunked the glass of milk down before her daughter, spilling a little. Again, Gabriella ignored the mess. Before Donovan died, she would have pointed out that Grace was perfectly capable of getting the milk herself and possibly made a sarcastic remark that the Milk Fairy had retired when Grace started second grade. But now, she just wordlessly sat back down but not before clearing her throat and raising her eyebrow meaningfully.

Grace looked confused for a second and then said, dully. "Oh, thank *you*."

"Hey, drop the attitude missy."

"Fine," Grace pushed back her chair and huffed out of the kitchen without touching the milk.

"Are you kidding me?" Gabriella said under her breath. At least most of the waffle was gone. As she stood to clear her daughter's place, she accidentally knocked over the still full glass of milk. It spread, seeping across the table and heading toward the floor. Meanwhile, in Gabriella's rush to stop the rolling glass from tumbling onto the floor and shattering, she sent a plate skidding off the edge. It fell, breaking into several sticky syrupy pieces on the terra cotta floor.

Her anger, which was always simmering just below the surface since Donovan's death, flared.

"Grace get in here this instant."

Nothing.

"Grace ... get in here right now." Her voice was hoarse and she could feel her face flush.

Grace stood with a smirk on her face in the doorway.

"I know things have been difficult for us, but that's no excuse. I will not allow you to be disrespectful. You will treat me with respect. You are acting like a spoiled brat."

The second the words poured out, Gabriella regretted them. Donovan had once told her that her temper was so ferocious that at times it seemed like lightning bolts were shooting from her eyes. At the time, they both thought it was funny.

Now, seeing the crushed look on Grace's face, Gabriella knew she had gone too far.

A tear slipped down Grace's cheek. She backed up, putting distance between her and her mother. Gabriella could tell her daughter was fighting back tears, clenching her teeth, blinking.

Instantly, all Gabriella's anger deflated. It was replaced with a hard pit of regret in her stomach. She took a step and reached for Grace, who shrunk back against the doorframe, as if her mother was a monster.

"Grace … I'm so sorry. You're not a spoiled brat. I don't believe in name-calling and I apologize. I don't always act the way I want to act and I was really out of line. Even when I'm upset that is no excuse for name calling."

Gabriella crouched down and reached for Grace's hand. Her daughter's skin was silk beneath her touch.

Grace jerked her arm away. The sadness from a moment ago was replaced by steely resolve. Grace didn't flinch as she spit the words out at her mother: "I. Hate. You."

She turned and ran through the penthouse into her bedroom,

slamming the door behind her.

CHAPTER FOUR

The sun was already warm and soothing on her bare arms and legs even though it was not yet noon. Stretched out poolside at her mother's Marin County ranch, Gabriella couldn't relax until she got her answer. She hadn't slept the night before so she kept her dark sunglasses on to disguise her dark circles. She'd been up all night worrying about Grace. Something needed to change. As dawn had crept over the Oakland Hills to the east, Gabriella got out of bed with determination. She knew what she needed to do to get her life back and be the mother her daughter needed.

But she was going to need her own mother's help.

Her request had been greeted with silence. She snuck a glance at her mother on the lawn chair beside her. Maria was biting her lip, thinking.

"Mama, please do this for me. I need to go. I need to see where he died. I need to say goodbye. If there is any way I can find him, I need to bring him back home," Gabriella stretched out her legs, pretending to examine a buckle on her sandals, but really trying to avoid her mother's eyes, afraid of what she might see there. "I need your help. I need you to stay with Grace while I'm gone. I won't be gone longer than a week. Two at the most."

Gabriella didn't mention that after yesterday's argument, her daughter probably wanted her to move to Central America for good.

She didn't blame Grace for being so upset. Parents were supposed to remain cool, calm, and collected. She'd blown that. She'd been out of line. Thinking of how she acted and what she said sent another stab of guilt through Gabriella. Everything was fucked up. She was a terrible mother and her husband was dead. She leaned back and closed her eyes.

She was going to do things differently. She had to. For Grace.

Today was the last day of Gabriella's bereavement leave. As the date to return to the newsroom had grown closer, Gabriella began to realize it was difficult to move past Donovan's death without a funeral, without a body, without some proof that he was gone—without at least an attempt to find him. She needed to go to where he died and say goodbye if she were ever going to move forward. Without doing that, without trying, she wasn't sure she could go back to work as a reporter. Her love for the crime beat seemed like a different life, a life that another person had lived.

Gabriella's mother reached over and squeezed her hand.

"Ella, if the United States government couldn't find Donovan what makes you think you can?"

Behind her dark sunglasses, Gabriella's eyes flew open. She couldn't think that way. She had to at least try to find Donovan or she'd never be able to move on. The thought of going back to work tomorrow, not knowing where his final resting place was, made her stomach hurt. She needed to go to Central America. She needed to do *something*, find something that would help her believe that Donovan truly was dead and that would allow her to find closure.

Her mother still wore her black hair in a sleek knot at the back of her head, but now it was streaked with striking strands of white at the front and sides. Her lips sported her signature red lipstick and her nails were painted a petal pink. She wore a loose white caftan over her one-piece black bathing suit. Her toned and tanned calves stuck out below, rivaling those of a woman twenty years younger. Her mother embodied *la bella figura*—the Italian art of always presenting your best face forward—like nobody else.

A maid appeared, handing them tall glasses of iced tea with fresh mint and red and white striped straws. Maria nodded at the woman like a queen, but Gabriella thanked the woman profusely.

She still hadn't gotten used to the opulence of her mother's new home—and new lifestyle. When her mother married Vincenzo

Santangelo, "The Saint," the long-time widow moved out of his penthouse in San Francisco and into his Marin County ranch full time. Then, six months ago, he "retired," saying he was going to spend the rest of his life making Maria happy.

He'd loved Maria since he was a teenager, he said. He claimed he wasn't ever going to let her out of his sight again and would dote on her until the day he died. So far that had involved taking Maria around the world to visit places she'd always dreamed about seeing, cooking her sumptuous meals, and basically making sure she didn't lift a finger.

Although Maria had hired a general manager for her flower shop in the East Bay, she'd insisted on working there every Saturday morning to keep tabs on how it was going. Meanwhile, she had acres of flowers, grape vines and vegetables to tend to here at the ranch when she felt like it. When she didn't, or when they were traveling, a team of gardeners supervised the bounty.

#

Both women looked toward the sparkling blue water in the pool, the late morning sunlight reflecting bright streaks of light onto their bare arms and faces.

The Saint was the best thing that had ever happened to her mother. He truly loved her. And he seemed to genuinely care about her children and grandchildren, treating them no differently than his own.

When the lease on Gabriella and Donovan's North Beach condo came up, he insisted they move into his vacant Nob Hill penthouse apartment. He told them it would be a big help. He needed to keep the place as an investment and didn't trust anyone else to live there. At first Donovan and Gabriella protested, but when he showed them the safe room and CIA-installed security and surveillance measures that included a private garage and elevator and the ability to push a button and have steel walls cover the penthouse windows, they conceded.

Nobody would ever get to Grace again. At least not when she was home in the penthouse. After they moved into the sky-high fortress, the seven-year-old confessed to her parents it was the first time she'd felt safe enough to sleep through the night since her abduction two years before.

Right then any guilt Gabriella felt about being "kept" by her mother's husband disappeared. She would do anything if it meant her daughter felt safe.

Now, Gabriella squinted at the sunlight reflecting in her face, hoping it was the brilliant light making her eyes tear up. "Mama, there has to be some signs of his plane crashing. It can't just disappear off the face of the earth without a trace. Not with today's technology."

"Amelia Earhart." Her mother said, clamping her lips together.

"It's different now. They can at least pinpoint where he was when they lost contact with him in Mexico. I'll start there."

"What? You put on your jogging shoes and start hiking through the jungle?" Maria said, tossing her hand up in the air. "That is absurd."

Gabriella looked away as she spoke. "I'll hire a guide. A native."

Maria sat up, peering at Gabriella over the top of her sunglasses.

"You are serious."

Gabriella took a long sip of her iced tea and nodded, slowly and emphatically. She kicked off her sandals, sending them tumbling onto the patio, one landed precariously next to the edge of the pool.

"I need to at least try."

Her mother stood up, gathered Gabriella's sandals, and placed them side-by-side beside the lounge chair.

Gabriella studied her mother. She looked too thin and suddenly fragile. She reminded herself that her mother was eighty. It wasn't easy to see her mother age. While she was still sharp, she was slower and seemed to nap a lot lately.

"Ma? You okay?"

Maria smiled and nodded without answering.

"I'm sorry for asking you to care for Grace. I know I sometimes take you for granted."

Her mother waved her hand and scoffed. "Don't be ridiculous. I love nothing more than spending time with my grandchildren. I would be happy to watch Grace for you. That is not what I'm talking about."

Gabriella felt water well in the corner of her eyes and she blinked rapidly to stem her tears. But her mother wasn't done speaking her mind.

"What if there is nothing? What if there is nothing to bring back home?"

Gabriella stood, tugged off her crocheted sweater and then slipped off her black shorts, revealing a tiny turquoise bikini. She folded her clothes in a neat pile by her sandals. Sitting on the edge of the lounge chair, she took her mother's hands in her own.

"I need to do this."

Her mother pressed her lips together tightly and nodded, blinking back tears. She reached over and patted her daughter's bare, tan leg. "*Andare con Dio.*" Go with God.

"Thanks, Mama." Gabriella leaned in and kissed her mother on the forehead and then leaned back, slipping her dark sunglasses over her eyes.

CHAPTER FIVE

A few years back, when Gabriella had exposed an elaborate cover-up involving 9/11, she'd had made a powerful ally in the state department.

That's why Senator Charles Corbin moved aside several appointments to accommodate her visit to D.C. that morning.

Gabriella strode into his office in a black suit with a calf-length skirt and Louboutin high-heeled black pumps. Her hair was pulled back into a tight bun and she wore only the lightest makeup. Capitol Hill dress code meant no nonsense.

"Mrs. Giovanni." He came out from around his oversize desk to pump her hand.

"Senator." Her grip was as firm as his. "Thank you so much for meeting with me on such short notice and thanks for your help last year on the book."

"My pleasure. I hope that forward I provided will work." He sat back down and pushed a folder across the desk to her. He didn't waste any time. "This folder contains your husband's itinerary for his trip to Central America, as near as we could figure it. The DEA fought like hell, but I think we were able to trace his movements from San Francisco until the plane disappeared in the jungle—we've narrowed it down with satellite images to a ten-mile square radius. I wish we could've done more or zeroed in closer, but something with the plane's nav system went awry. And the jungle canopy really makes it tough to see what's happening on the ground."

He paused and watched her face.

Gabriella nodded. A ten-mile radius would work. She studied the paperwork in her lap. It would not be an easy journey. Feeling his gaze on her, Gabriella looked up and caught something in the senator's eyes. Something dangerous, some type of warning. He knew something about the trip he wasn't telling her.

"Is there something else?" The hairs on her arm rose as she waited.

The senator looked as if he was about to say something. His eyes had narrowed just slightly and he opened his mouth. Then the phone rang. He stood. "I'm sorry, that's my signal that my committee is meeting to vote, but I wanted to make sure you got this information."

Again, he paused, examining her. What wasn't he telling her? Then he was at the door holding it open.

Gabriella offered her hand before she left. "You've been extremely helpful. I won't forget it."

She was halfway down the hallway when he called her name. She turned.

"Be careful."

She nodded and he turned and walked the other way. She watched until he disappeared around a corner, his broad shoulders in his expensive suit exuding a poise, confidence, and authority that on politicians seemed natural.

In the Town Car driving to the airport, Gabriella clutched the folder on her lap. She didn't want to let go of it, even to put it in her shoulder bag. The senator had come up with the information overnight and then made room to see her on her whirlwind visit.

But he knew something, probably something upsetting or dangerous that he wasn't telling her. He had been about to tell her of something, but instead left it with a wishy-washy warning to "be careful."

Brushing her apprehension aside, Gabriella felt grateful that she had the senator in her corner. This trip wouldn't be possible without this information he'd provided and the hurdles he had cleared, acting like a tour director to plan every leg of her trip even down to hiring the guide. She appreciated how he referred to Donovan as her husband—in the present tense—and how he didn't say the plane had crashed.

"Disappeared" was the right term. Until she found the wreckage, that is how she viewed it, as well.

Because in the deep, darkest of night, she clung to the tiniest shred of hope that Donovan wasn't dead. She didn't want to believe it completely until she saw the wreckage, found some trace of him. Maybe even found his body. That might be what it would take. Otherwise it was too hard to not believe it was all a mistake.

Right now, her heart wouldn't let her believe he was gone. Back home in San Francisco, there were brief moments—just whispered breaths during her day— where it was too easy to believe he was out of the country on business. He'd return home to her and Grace, his quiet, yet powerful personality back home infusing the penthouse with a feeling of safety and warmth that only he could provide.

CHAPTER SIX

Gabriella stared out her windshield at the big brick façade of the *Bay Herald*. Her palms were slick and her heart pounded in her ears. She could feel a headache forming over her right eye.

For so many years this had been her home away from home. But right now, she was terrified to enter its doors. A series of images flashed through her mind that had nothing to do with the newspaper building in front of her.

Snapshots of Donovan when they first met. He was the sexy cop at the crime scene. She was the reporter trying to get him to tip her off to the real story.

She'd cried in this newsroom. She'd been questioned by homicide detectives in this building. She'd even made love to Donovan once down by the mammoth printing presses, her back against a wall, her groans inaudible next to the deafening noise of the Sunday print run in full force.

The newspaper building was more familiar than her own home. It held so many memories, but every ounce of her being wanted to turn the key in the ignition and race back to San Francisco.

Last night as they hugged goodbye, her mother had suggested that Gabriella consider quitting her job. But she wasn't ready to do that. At least not yet.

It wasn't about the money. Although Donovan's salary had been meager and Gabriella's leave was unpaid, she didn't really need to work.

The Saint wouldn't allow them to pay any rent on the penthouse and their expenses were very low. However, if she quit her job as a reporter, as her mother had been begging her to do for years, Gabriella would lose her independence. Gone. Kaput.

And she'd lose her identity. While being a mother was the most important and best job in the world, she needed more.

Her editor, Matt Kellogg, needed to let her do this one last thing and then she could get back to her life as a reporter. Then this crawling feeling that made her want to run away would hopefully disappear.

Gabriella made the sign of the cross. Please let Kellogg understand how important this was to her. He usually came in around nine. It was 9:30, so he should be there already. Gabriella watched as a few people filtered into the newsroom door. Nobody noticed her sitting in her car.

Finally, she opened her car door.

CHAPTER SEVEN

The newsroom grew silent as Gabriella entered. She headed straight toward Kellogg's desk. She ignored the whispering and the few heads that popped up to watch her journey past features, sports, and into the metro section. She was worried if she made eye contact with any of her friends and colleagues, she would burst into tears.

She stood at the side of Kellogg's desk, waiting until he looked up.

His smile stretched across his face and she blinked to keep the tears at bay.

"The ace is back!"

This would be harder than she thought.

"Can we talk in the conference room for a minute?" She swallowed and looked away.

A frown creased his brow. "Of course." He stood, knocking some books over on his desk.

On the way to the conference room, a few people greeted Gabriella. She tried to smile, but failed. They passed the librarian Liz who blew a kiss at Gabriella, but then when Liz saw Kellogg's face she pouted. Gabriella gave her a weak smile.

As soon as the door to the conference room closed, Kellogg leaned back against it.

"You're not handing in your notice. I refuse to accept it."

"I'm not quitting. But I need more time off. Two weeks. Maybe three."

Gabriella pretended not to notice that each time she brought up the trip to someone, the length of time she planned to be gone increased.

He frowned. "Of course, I want to let you, but the big boss has already bitched about the leave I gave you. Nobody has ever received a two-month leave. May has been working your beat like a champ, but if you are gone any longer, she's going to take it over permanently. You'll get kicked to the night cops position. And just so you know, you guys may get along fine, but May is *not* your friend. She's been vying for your job since she walked in this place years ago and she's not ready to give up yet. In fact, I should tell you that this conversation— about her taking over your beat full-time—this is a conversation that May's already had with the publisher. It would be hard for me to argue your side. She scooped the shit out of the Helzer's story and the Dutton kidnapping case."

Gabriella nodded. She was prepared. She'd thought long and hard about how to handle it.

"Give her my beat."

Kellogg raised an eyebrow and started to speak, but Gabriella raised her palm.

"Hear me out. We both know she's earned it. Make me an investigative reporter. I know you guys haven't replaced Simmerman yet. I mean, God knows, nobody could truly replace him. But give me his beat. I've got the first story to pitch. About the Cartel filtering drugs here, right to the suburban homes in Pleasant Valley. I'm going to Central America to do the reporting. I'll try to interview some of the minor players in the drug war. I'll file a story every other day while I'm gone. And then at the end, have a Sunday spread about my project. You know I can do this."

"I don't like what I'm hearing." He crossed his arms across his chest.

"What?" Gabriella ignored what he was implying.

"As your editor, I think it's a kick ass idea. As your friend, I think you are setting yourself up for more grief—and by my estimation, you've already had a lifetime's worth of grief times ten. You are sabotaging the life you have. You are forgetting that you have a little girl who just lost her dad and now you're going to leave her and go gallivanting around trying to interview drug lords. She doesn't need to lose her mom now, too."

The tears she'd been holding back were now dripping down her cheeks.

When he saw that, a look of horror spread across his face.

"Fuck that came out wrong." He leaned down and tried to hug her but she shrugged away, wiping at her tears with her sleeve.

Being a reporter meant hearing harsh things from editors without being a wuss about it, but this one stung. "It's okay. I know what you're trying to say," she said in a stuffed-up voice.

"I'm sorry if I crossed the line there, but I'm not talking to you as your editor. I'm talking to you as your friend," Kellogg said. "I'm worried about you."

Gabriella straightened up and met his eyes. "I know what I'm doing."

He waited a few seconds staring at her and then pressed his lips together tightly and nodded.

"Fine. You got it," he stood and held open the door. "I expect your first story filed in two weeks."

CHAPTER EIGHT

The small plane bucked and weaved and sent a wave of nausea through Gabriella, but it couldn't tamp down the excitement she felt seeing the roof of the jungle below her. For the first time in months she felt alive again. Instead of sitting around helplessly mourning her husband's death, she was doing something.

The crackle of the pilot's voice in her headphones startled her.

"Prepare for landing."

She gave her seatbelt an unnecessary tug and leaned back, rubbing the blue and silver image of the Virgin Mary on her miraculous medal—a superstitious gesture she made when she was nervous. The most dangerous part of the flight was before them. The pilot was going to attempt to land on a short dirt landing strip in a tiny clearing surrounded by the rainforest. A miscalculation could send them careening into the thick jungle canopy. If the plane crashed and she died, Grace would be an orphan. It would be too improbable for Grace to lose both her parents in Central American plane crashes. It would be too cruel.

They'd taken off from Guatemala City forty-five minutes ago.

Soon, the small clearing appeared below. It looked like a football field,

not a landing strip, but within seconds the small plane had dipped and

was whizzing by rusted cars and a small building on the side of the

runway below. The plane was still rocking from side to side, as the

pilot attempted to keep it level despite the wind.

Gabriella peered out the window, not sure what she was

looking for. This was where Donovan had landed when he first came to

Central America. This was also where his last flight had taken off.

Besides the tiny clearing before them, it was thick jungle for as far as

she could see.

Gazing out the window, Gabriella searched for ghostly trails of

where Donovan had once been, imagining him in a plane like hers.

Imagining him in this seat taking in the surroundings, a patch of cleared

land smack in the middle of the jungle. She ached for any sign of his

presence, lingering in the ether, even though she knew it was futile and

a little ridiculous. Although she didn't really believe Donovan left

traces of himself behind, Gabriella couldn't help but feel closer to him

here, where he had been only days before his death.

From this point on, her path would deviate from his. While his

plane landed here simply to refuel before continuing its journey to

another airstrip further inland and close to a top-secret DEA fortress, she would trace the plane's path on the ground. It was the only way to access the ten-mile radius in the jungle surrounding the satellite coordinates showing where Donovan's plane was last heard from.

Letting go of the miraculous medal around her neck, she thought of Grace. She'd given her daughter an identical medal before she left the United States yesterday. Grace had rolled her eyes, something Gabriella pretended not to see. Her daughter was still angry—about their argument, but also plain angry at the world. The same way Gabriella was. Maria had promised to take Grace to her therapy sessions while Gabriella was gone. Hopefully, it would help and when Gabriella returned, things would be better. It broke her heart that she had caused Grace any more pain. Regret was not something Gabriella was used to feeling.

She jolted back to the present when she realized the aircraft was only feet above the dirt landing strip.

With a whisper light touch, the back wheels touched solid ground. A second later, the front wheels met the runway and the aircraft glided until it hit a patch of gravel, which signaled they had gone past the end of the runway. Gabriella clutched at the seat in front of her until the plane skidded to a stop only ten feet away from the thick trees of the jungle.

"Sorry about that, mate." The pilot's Australian accent filled her headphones. "That tailwind got the best of me." Gabriella looked up and saw the pilot smiling at her in the round rearview mirror. Instead of answering, she took off her headphones and gave him the thumbs up signal. He got her here in one piece. That was all that mattered.

Gathering her large leather backpack and a small bag with her laptop and a power cord, she hopped out of the plane. She'd told Kellogg it looked like she wouldn't be able to file as often as she'd promised. Since she would be so deep in the jungle, she'd take notes on her trip and then file a large Sunday story from the airport in two weeks.

She wore black cargo pants, a black tank top, and hiking boots. She had bought three pairs of the pants, six of the tank tops and a lightweight jacket peppered with zippered pockets. Other than sunscreen, bug spray, and lip balm, the only toiletries she carried were soap, toothpaste, and a small first aid kit. She'd wash her hair with the soap and then put it back up in a ponytail. She was packing everything on her back. There was no room for anything except necessities.

Besides, the way she looked was the furthest thing from her mind. It seemed a lifetime away that she had gone on an extravagant shopping spree— buying sexy lingerie, bikinis, and sundresses for her

vacation to Jamaica with Donovan. The one that never happened.

This trip she couldn't even be bothered with tinted lip balm.

This was not a vacation. She was here to find her husband's dead body.

CHAPTER NINE

Her guide, Rafael, waited by a beat-up Jeep at the edge of the airstrip.

"Miss Giovanni?" he asked, walking up and sticking out his hand. He was shorter than her five foot six inches but he was thick and strong with meaty arms and a barrel chest. His calves were all muscle below his shorts. He had a thin mustache and solemn black eyes.

"Mrs." She shook hands with him grimly, matching his tone. This wasn't about making friends or charming the locals.

"We will leave in five minutes," he said. "There is a bathroom if you need it." He pointed to the small building. Gabriella shook her head. They stood and watched the pilot taxi down the runway. It didn't seem he would ever gain enough speed to become airborne. But somehow, he did and even managed to tip his hat to her and grin as he lifted into the air in front of them.

She waited until the plane had cleared the trees before she tossed her bags into the backseat, tugged an Army green baseball cap low over her eyes and hopped into the passenger seat.

Rafael smiled for the first time and revved the engine. *"Vamos!"*

Gabriella nodded without taking her eyes off the windshield.

He didn't ask questions and Gabriella didn't volunteer information. Because the senator arranged for Rafael to be her guide, Gabriella assumed this meant Rafael knew why she was here and what she wanted. He was to take her through the jungle to the spot where Donovan's plane was last heard from. The ancient Mayan city of Uaxactun would serve as home base while she took day trips to search a ten-mile radius around the target location. DEA officials estimated that at that point in the flight, the plane would've reappeared on radar or satellite if it had made it past that ten-mile circle. Still, extensive searches of that area had yielded nothing. Gabriella didn't understand. A part of her suspected that the DEA had claimed to search the area to appease the families of the victims, but truly had just written lost men off without even trying to find the bodies.

As they drove deeper into the jungle, the trees formed an even thicker canopy above the dirt road, blocking out the sun. The sounds of the wildlife grew louder.

Birds shrieking and whistling and then a sound of something fierce growling, like a large monster, the fierce roar echoing through the trees.

"Good God, what the hell is that?" She shouted over the Jeep's engine.

Rafael laughed. "A Howler monkey."

"A monkey? You're telling me that monster sound is a little monkey?"

He nodded.

Gabriella searched the branches above and the thick trees to the side, looking for some of the creatures making the strange noises, but they were so well camouflaged, all she saw was the lush greenery.

The constant buzz of tiny insects made Gabriella grateful for the bug spray she'd lathered on at the airstrip. Even though they never landed on her body, the small gnats and some larger insects she didn't recognize swarmed around her head. She was afraid if she said anything, she'd accidently inhale a posse of them.

Keeping her mouth closed, she scanned the jungle around her, awed by the lush tropical terrain.

Even though it made her feel guilty, it felt exhilarating to be in a rainforest she'd only read about. It also felt good to finally do something about Donovan's disappearance. She was still reluctant to say "his death."

Disappearance was less permanent. It appeared that small

tendril of hope she nurtured that he had somehow survived the plane

crash and was still somewhere in this jungle. It wasn't so far-fetched.

Unfolding the map that she'd marked up in San Francisco,

Gabriella tried to locate where they were in their dense jungle.

Somewhere between the airstrip and their first stop—a village where

they would ask about Donovan and she'd pass out the fliers with his

face and description. Consulting her crude map, Gabriella saw that it

led inland, away from the coast.

#

The village was about twenty miles from the airport, but

because of the dirt road filled with car-sized potholes, it took them

nearly an hour to get there. The "village" ended up being about half a

dozen small huts lining the dirt road. Chickens roamed everywhere –

on the tin metal roofs and all over the road. They had to stop and wait

for the chickens to haphazardly wander off the road, oblivious to the

Jeep. It was only when Rafael honked that they finally got out of the

way.

They parked next to a beat-up 1970 Ford truck. With the

engine turned off, the jungle surrounding them was noisy with bird

song and strange clicking and scrabbling noises she couldn't identify.

"Wait here," Rafael said and headed toward the buildings. A few men sat in plastic chairs tucked under the eaves of the buildings out of the sun.

Gabriella leaned against the hot metal side of the Jeep and watched Rafael approach one man on a nicer chair than the others. His chair was wicker with a plump flowered cushion. The man was squat and despite the heat wore a brightly colored embroidered poncho. A giant straw hat and sunglasses hid most of his face.

While Gabriella watched, a clump of noisy chickens approached her, looking to be fed. She tried to ignore them but they kept getting closer, looking up at her every once in a while.

When one of them picked at the shoelace to her boot, she leaned down and hissed, "Go away" and waved her arms, but they ignored her. Finally, she nudged one of them with her foot and it went rushing away in a flurry of feathers and outraged squawking. The others soon followed, darting white-eyed glances at her as they left.

The man in the poncho didn't appear to say much from what Gabriella could see. He nodded a few times in response to whatever Rafael was saying and occasionally leaned over to expertly spit some chewing tobacco juice into an old-fashioned spittoon by his chair. When the chickens headed his way, he leaned down into a small tin can and spread seed for them to peck at near his feet. About a dozen chickens swarmed him, clucking loudly. He caught Gabriella's eye and winked. She nodded back.

The sun was high in the sky now and she could feel its warmth beating down on the top of her head even with her baseball cap on. Small beads of sweat dripped from her temples. Swarms of tiny insects circled her, but most seemed more interested in a small fire pit piled with food scraps. Finally, tired of standing and roasting in the sun, she crouched down by the Jeep in the dirt, squatting in a small patch of shade. The air was thick, heavy with moisture, pressing down on her, making it hard to breathe.

The sound of a small plane made her look up. It looked like a private jet. She wondered where it had come from and where it was heading. It seemed out of place in this wilderness as it zoomed overhead. The old man in the wicker chair looked up, too, shading his eyes. Not taking his eyes off the sky, he said something in Spanish and then spit on the ground in disgust.

Rafael looked up too and then shrugged. The man finally returned his gaze to Rafael and the conversation resumed.

Finally, Gabriella saw Rafael thrust a wad of green bills at the man, who waved it away and gestured to a small boy who grabbed the money and ran.

Rafael hopped back into the vehicle.

"He says we can pass freely now. The rebels will allow us past their checkpoint."

Gabriella didn't ask who the old man was and Rafael didn't volunteer. Apparently, this crappy, pothole filled dirt road taking them deeper into the jungle had an entrance fee. If they didn't pay the price, they wouldn't get far. The man in front of the hut somehow had some control of what happened further into the jungle. As they pulled away, Gabriella gave one last glance back at the man to see if he was going to get up to make a phone call or pull a radio out of his pocket telling someone down the road that Rafael and Gabriella had paid to be unmolested. But when she turned, she saw he had pulled the brim of his hat low over his face and was leaning his head back against the building. His chest rose and fell heavily, as if he had immediately dropped into a deep sleep.

Nothing in Gabriella's thick sheaf of documents mentioned these types of roadblocks. Once again, she was relieved the senator had made the arrangements for her journey through his official channels.

About a mile out of the small village, the road split into three directions. Rafael took the road to the far left. The road instantly curved and they'd gone only about a quarter mile when she saw them. Five men dressed in khaki camouflage standing in the middle of the road with what looked like a machine gun. The rebels.

CHAPTER TEN

Off to the side of the road was a small shack. Smoke rose from a fire pit and Gabriella could smell charred meat. Five chairs were gathered around the fire and several cans of beer with condensation were scattered on stumps that served as end tables. A small table held a few bowls of food and some tortillas. They'd heard the Jeep coming and had interrupted their lunch to greet them. If that is what they were doing.

Rafael stopped the Jeep well before they got close to the men. One man, with a tiny moustache and military cap, approached, holding the gun out in front of him, aimed at Rafael, his finger on the trigger. A second man wearing a black tank top with his khaki combat fatigues, trailed behind him, pointing his gun at Gabriella. He was not smiling. For a second, Gabriella was convinced she was going to die. Her heart pounded wildly in her throat. She was so stupid to have come out here.

Rafael slowly put both of his hands straight up in the air until the man reached the side of the Jeep.

"*La noche está cerca.*" Rafael said as soon as the man was close. The night is near.

The man nodded. It must have been some type of password.

By this time, the gunman on Gabriella's side had reached her door. He slung his gun down by his side and reached in, gently rubbing his rough finger down her cheek. She stared straight ahead out the windshield.

From doing stories with the gang investigators in Hunter's Point, San Francisco's most dangerous neighborhood, she'd learned not to make eye contact with gang members. She figured the same rule applied out here.

After stroking her cheek for a second and mumbling something in Spanish she didn't understand, the man started to trail his hand down her neck and to her chest. When his fingers reached the scooped top of her tank top, she finally turned her head to Rafael, desperate. She was fighting her instinct to slap the guy across the face. The other gunman, who had been flipping through Rafael's wallet, saw what his *compadre* was doing and said something sharply in Spanish. The man instantly drew back. The man with the hat threw Rafael's wallet onto the seat between them, whistled piercingly and backed off.

Hearing the whistle, the other men moved off to the side of the road.

Rafael started the car and was about to step on the gas when the gunman told him to stop. He'd spotted the small ice chest in the back of the Jeep. He reached in and flipped it open, grabbed a bottle of amber

liquid and then waved them on.

As they passed the gunman on the side of the road, Gabriella

felt a chill run down her arms even though she was sweating from the

heat. They gunmen looked like teenage boys. They stared, black eyes

expressionless, until the Jeep had passed.

After a few minutes when they were about a mile past the

checkpoint, Rafael reached back into the cooler behind the seat and

handed Gabriella a dented tin canteen full of water.

"So, what? He takes my tequila? Big whoop," Rafael said,

clearly irritated. "But we have more important thing still—the water.

Tequila you can buy here cheap. Water? Is much harder to find in the

jungle."

She gratefully chugged on it, while he took a long sip of his

own canteen before wiping the sweat dripping down his brow with a

blue bandanna he untied from his neck.

They drove away, neither one of them mentioning the

encounter with the rebels, but Gabriella's heart was still racing. Rafael

seemed unfazed by it.

Even after she had calmed down, Gabriella was perspiring like

mad. The sweat pooled in the small pocket under her tank top between

her breasts. Gabriella poured a tiny bit of water in her palm and then splashed it on her face. Rafael gave her a sideways glance she immediately understood. She remembered what he said about it being hard to find water. It was not to be wasted.

Chastened, she screwed the lid back on and tucked the canteen between her knees.

Gabriella scanned the thick jungle closing in on the road, looking for signs of life. Animals. People. Anything. In her imagination, the Jeep would round a corner and there they'd find Donovan, bruised and battered, maybe with blood-soaked bandages and torn clothing, but alive.

She was jolted out of her daydream by Rafael slamming on the brakes and skidding to a stop. A bloody carcass with strips of torn meat and bones was scattered across the road in front of them.

"Did you see it?"

Gabriella's eyes were wide as she shook her head. She'd been looking off to the other side and didn't see anything.

"A jaguar. It ran that way when we came around the corner."

She nodded, peering into the thick jungle, looking for a spotted coat and glowing eyes. She hugged herself as a chill ran across her scalp, feeling cold and exposed in her tank top in the door less Jeep.

Standing up in the Jeep, peering across the hood, she tried to figure out what the bloody mess in front of the Jeep once was.

"Tapir." Rafael said.

Gabriella shrugged.

He scrunched his face and then said, "Like a big pig, but with nose like an anteater."

Gabriella nodded. It must have been big. There was blood and guts and flesh everywhere. Once again, she glanced around the jungle surrounding them. That cat wasn't done with his dinner yet.

She was relieved when, without ceremony Rafael stepped on the gas pedal and accelerated across the bloody carcass, bumping along as if it were a pothole and not a creature that had been alive until moments ago.

After a while, the canopy above them seemed to diminish, with more sunlight filtering down on the road. Not long after that, when they'd been on the road about an hour, the Jeep popped out of the jungle and into a clearing with smaller trees and brush. The sunlight beat down on Gabriella's bare arms and the top of her ball cap.

About a mile ahead, between the trees, she saw the outline of small brown buildings. It was the outpost she'd seen on her map.

Rounding a corner, she saw there was a small dirt parking lot in front of the two buildings. Along with a rusted pick-up truck, a sleek black late model Range Rover was parked in the lot. Rafael leaned forward swearing under his breath.

"Who is it?" Gabriella said.

"This guy. He wanted to hire me this morning to take him to Uaxactun, but I told him I already was taking you." Rafael said. "I would not work for him anyway. He is … something off. I don't know how to say it. In Spanish, we say *me da mala espinas*." He hugged himself and shivered.

Gabriella nodded. Without knowing the Spanish, she understood. The guy gave Rafael the creeps.

Gabriella reached for her backpack as the Jeep pulled into the outpost.

Several men wearing big straw hats sat on a bench out front, sipping cans of beer and spitting tobacco onto the ground. A few boys who looked to be middle school kicked a ball around in the dirt behind one of the buildings.

"They are on recess."

"This is a school?"

"Consuela and her daughter, Marta, teach the boys English in the afternoons, after the boys work in the fields all morning. Those men are their fathers and grandfathers who have dropped them off at the school and are sharing a *cerveza* and village gossip before siesta starts.

"Where do they all live?"

Rafael waved wildly, gesturing somewhere to the right. It didn't make sense to her, but maybe there were homes tucked into the dense forest.

Within the hour, Rafael said, the men would lie on folded up mats in the shade of a large tree until the boys were done with their English classes, Rafael explained. They gathered here every day, which is why it would be a good place to ask about Donovan.

Rafael thumbed through a stack of American dollar bills, peeling off about twenty of them. He shoved the smaller stack in his front shirt pocket, tucked the larger stack deep into his jeans pocket, and grabbed a stack of the fliers. He told Gabriella to go inside and order something to eat. He would have better luck questioning the men if he were alone. She nodded.

Gabriella swung her legs out of the Jeep. The front door, a tattered screen with bells, opened and a man wearing a crisp white shirt with the sleeves rolled up and khaki pants and dark sunglasses stepped out. A long scar ran down his cheek.

The Italian from Josephine Lake.

CHAPTER ELEVEN

The Italian's eyes were impossible to see behind his dark glasses so Gabriella couldn't tell if his smile was genuine. He took both her hands in his. She caught a whiff of his expensive cologne. Again, she stared at the scar, wondering how he had got it.

"*Ciao bella. Mi chiamo* Nico Sicilia. I'm afraid we didn't have time to get introduced the last time we saw each other."

"Gabriella Giovanni." She said it with brisk efficiency. She planned to say as little as possible until she figured out what was going on and he explained why he was in the deepest jungle of Central America driving a Range Rover.

"It seems maybe we are on parallel paths," he said with a smile that revealed perfect white teeth.

She nodded waiting.

"If I had known you would be here, I would've waited to eat lunch. I am unaccustomed to dining alone. Ah, but maybe next time. Meanwhile, I would recommend the empanadas. Oh, and the *senorita* also cooks amazing tamales."

He held his thumb and fingers together and kissed them, a very Italian gesture. It was sexy and remembering her reaction to his scar, she shifted uncomfortably. The only person she wanted to find sexy was her husband, the love of her life. She reminded herself that this guy gave Rafael the creeps. Gabriella didn't want to show an ounce of warmth toward him until she figured out why.

And besides, in only a few seconds, he had already lied to her about not knowing she was there. Rafael told him this morning that she'd hired him. Plus, she didn't want to admit that the shivers he gave her a moment ago had nothing to do with being creeped out. The opposite, in fact.

He continued to stare at her. Even though she couldn't see behind his dark glasses, she could feel his gaze. When neither spoke for several seconds, she finally caved.

"What brings you to Guatemala?"

"I'm here for my government."

"In what capacity?"

"I handle covert operations. Things I am not at liberty to discuss."

"Covert operations involving the cartel, of course," Gabriella said. "But that still doesn't explain why you are here at this outpost right now."

After more than a decade as a reporter, she wasn't going to accept his evasive answers that easily.

"I'm heading to Uaxactun. Same as you."

Aha. A sliver of honesty. She rewarded him with a smile.

It seemed like it made him nervous because he stumbled a little over his next words. "We could caravan if you like. My driver will wait until your business is finished here."

For a second, the aura of confidence seemed to dim a little as if he knew the answer already.

"No, thank you." Gabriella brushed by him and tugged on the screen door, letting it slam behind her without a backward glance.

Inside, a squat woman with dark hair pulled back in a thick braid gave Gabriella a giant smile and gestured to a small table by the door.

"*Buenas tardes*," she said.

Gabriella smiled as she settled into the red plastic chair.

The small room only had three tables, but each one had a clean white tablecloth, white napkins, silverware and a tiny vase with a small flower in it.

The woman brought a plastic cup of water. "*Qué te gusta?*" What would you like?

Her Spanish was rusty so she shrugged and pointed at the woman repeating the words back to her, *"Qué te gusta."*

She hoped it translated back to something like "I'll have what you like to eat."

The woman stared at her for a second and then understood, nodding and smiling, running her palms down her apron as she walked back to the kitchen whistling.

Gabriella's mouth watered from the smell of some type of meat simmering in a large pot on the counter. On a small griddle the woman was heating up a stack of tortillas.

After a few moments, she brought over some tortillas, refried beans, white rice and chunks of meat smothered in some sort of chili sauce. She hesitated and Gabriella smiled. Perfect.

She dug in, piling beans and rice and meat in the tortilla, folding it carefully and taking a bite. She closed her eyes with happiness. When she opened them, she caught the woman watching. She put her hands on her heart in a gesture of gratefulness and pleasure. The woman blushed with pleasure and bustled around cleaning while Gabriella finished the first tortilla and started to fill a second one.

When the door opened, Gabriella didn't look up from her food, expecting Rafael to slide into the seat opposite her. Instead, she smelled that same cologne. She knew who it was before her eyes traveled up the man's body. The Italian.

He crouched down so they were eye level and took off his sunglasses. Gabriella was startled by the color of his eyes. Not many Italians had eyes that icy blue. They were striking against his dark skin.

"I came in to apologize for being so vague and unhelpful," he said and quickly looked around. The woman had disappeared into the kitchen. "It's the *Omerta*. You must know what that means, right? You do have ancestors from Italy, I assume."

"I know what *Omerta* means," Gabriella said, not flinching from his gaze. "And I know people use it as an excuse to keep secrets."

He smiled at her curt tone. And shrugged, as if conceding. But Gabriella knew every word was calculated. Whatever came out of his mouth next, she knew he had planned on what to say before he walked in the door.

"There is a man I need to find. Someone who is very dangerous to our undercover operation here in Guatemala. My job is to find him and make sure our cover is not blown. I am not allowed to speak about it because if they even get an inkling that we might have an operative undercover here, I am effectively signing his death warrant. Do you understand why I must be careful about who I share this information with?"

"I'm also looking for a man." Gabriella said in a small voice, looking away.

"Your husband. Sean Donovan."

She was startled, even though she knew she shouldn't be. She nodded.

"They said his plane went down near the Northern border of Guatemala," she said. "That's why I'm heading to Uaxactun."

"I know. The man I am looking for was on that plane."

Now, she really was surprised.

"So, we are looking for the same thing?"

"I believe so."

Gabriella kicked out a chair with one booted foot. "Have a seat, Mr. Silicia."

"Nico."

"I'm going to ask around in the small villages. There are a lot of small ranches, tucked away in the jungle, mostly run by people hired by the cartel. It is dangerous to start asking questions, but it may be my best bet. If you like, I will also ask about your husband. But first I need to go to El Mirador first to pick up some guns. I've arranged for the purchase of two weapons. It was too difficult to try to bring them into the country, but it appears easy enough to buy them once you are here. Money talks, as they say."

He looked at her. "What is your plan?"

Gabriella shrugged. She wasn't sure she wanted to share.

"You know this is not America," he said. "These people kill as easily as they scratch an itch. You need a cover. With Rafael as your guide, you could easily claim to be an environmental reporter studying the rainforest. You have reporter's credentials with you, correct?"

Gabriella nodded, thinking of the press pass with her photo tucked deep in her bag.

"They won't kill you for that. For reporting. At least I don't think so."

"That's comforting."

When she was done eating, she left a twenty-dollar bill on the counter and headed outside to where Rafael was waiting in the driver's seat of the Jeep. Nico trailed behind her, settling into his own vehicle.

When she had walked out of the small café and Rafael had seen her with Nico, he had spit out the open door of the Jeep.

Gabriella gestured toward the Range Rover.

"They are going to follow us. We are all heading to the same place, after all."

Rafael shook his head but didn't say anything, just turned the key in the ignition.

Too bad. It was her dollar. Rafael wasn't showing her around for free. She was paying him to do what she asked, so he'd have to deal with Nico, even if he didn't like him.

After he started the engine, Rafael told her in a low voice that he'd had no luck with the men out in front of the small kitchen. He said one guy knew something but wasn't talking. He could tell by the look in his eyes.

"You should let me talk to him," Gabriella unbuckled her seatbelt, but Rafael held his arm across her. "He may be a lead for us. I paid one of the schoolboys to follow him after the siesta. He will see who he speaks to and then let Marta in the kitchen know about he finds. It is better if the man does not know we are onto him or he may realize the boy is following him."

Gabriella settled back in her seat, heart pounding. Rafael was right, even if all she wanted to do was shake the man's shoulders until he told her what he knew.

"Wait and make sure Nico's vehicle is behind us," Gabriella said, watching the driver lope over to the Range Rover.

As they pulled away from the outpost, Rafael glared at the rearview mirror and swore under his breath in Spanish.

CHAPTER TWELVE

They were only a few miles away from the outpost when the road began to climb. The road was winding around a small hill. Suddenly, the one-lane dirt road narrowed even more and the ground dropped away on one side. As Rafael rounded a corner, a giant tree lay across their path. On one side was a fifteen-foot drop. On the other, the side of the mountain. There was no way they could drive around it.

Gabriella and Rafael got out and tugged at the fallen tree, but were only able to roll it a few inches before it rolled right back into place. Despite Rafael's muscles, they couldn't lift it more than a few inches. The Range Rover pulled up behind them and the Italian and his guide came over and wordlessly began to tug at the tree.

As he lifted the tree, seemingly effortlessly, Nico glanced at Gabriella.

"Did you know Guatemala, was originally called Goathemala, which means 'Land of trees?'" he said.

"Makes sense to me," she said, huffing, trying to hold up the smaller end of the tree to help.

Finally, with the four of them pushing and pulling, they were able to shove the tree off to the side, clearing enough of the road for the vehicles to pass. Gabriella thanked Nico and his guide, but Rafael ignored them and climbed back into the Jeep, taking off before the other two men had even returned to the Range Rover.

Gabriella shot a look his way. "So, it was sort of a good idea they were behind us, wasn't it?"

Rafael stared straight ahead and grunted, a sour look on his face.

At nightfall, they pulled down a small driveway that led to what could be considered a motel. Nico and Gabriella waited by the vehicles in the dark while their guides negotiated the price for four small bedrooms. The two-story structure was home to the family downstairs and then stairs from the parking lot led to an outside walkway with four rooms.

Inside, Gabriella's small room was little more than a bed with a mosquito net over it. The room didn't have electricity, only a candle. It also only had three walls. The fourth wall, which had a flimsy screen and waist-high wall, opened to the jungle, which was only twenty feet away. Gabriella threw her backpack under the bed's mosquito netting and shivered, hearing the jungle start to come alive as darkness fell harder around them. It sounded like the animals were right outside her room, which was still ten feet above the ground, but seemed accessible by anything that was used to climbing trees. Inside her room, a small door led to a sink and toilet. No bath or shower.

The group had agreed to meet back outside and prepare dinner in the parking lot by their cars. The owner of the motel—if that's what it was supposed to be—had lit a small campfire out front and propped four stumps around it for them to sit on.

When Gabriella came back outside, Rafael and Nico's guide, Cristo, were busy behind the Jeep heating their dinner of beans and rice on a small kerosene stove. Cristo had contributed some pork sausages to the dinner. When Rafael saw them, it was the first time Gabriella had seen him smile like that. Maybe he'd finally get over being mad at her for wanting to travel with Nico and his guide.

"What the hell is up with the wall open to the jungle? Is this place for people who have a death wish? A sort of suicide camp or something?" Gabriella asked, plopping onto a stump.

Nico gestured at the building behind them, ignoring Gabriella's sarcasm and grumpiness. "It is an eco-tourist site. I saw it on Lonely Planet. Rich socialites in Manhattan pay big bucks to sleep in those rooms we are in."

"You gotta be kidding."

"Not kidding."

"The difference is those people, the upper-class ones, you could say, travel with guides who drive small motor homes. The vehicles have showers and kitchens. If the missus doesn't want the whole jungle experience, she can sleep in the motorhome that night. But they can always go home and talk about their wild adventures sleeping in a room with one wall that is the jungle."

"They maneuver motor homes through those jungle roads like we took today?"

Nico nodded. "They are smaller, much smaller than you probably think. Would only really sleep one person or two at the most."

"Motorhome, huh?" Gabriella said, squinting at large parking spaces in front of the hotel with the hookups for electricity that now finally made sense. "That's really roughing it."

A few minutes later the four of them ate beans and rice and sausage. After they were done, Gabriella offered to wash the dishes.

Rafael put out his hand. "All included. Meals, clean up. All by me."

"Well thank you."

After he walked away, Gabriella excused herself to grab her jacket out of her room.

CHAPTER THIRTEEN

When Gabriella returned, Nico was alone.

"Your man and Cristo have turned in," he said.

"Tomorrow we should reach Uaxactun," she said taking a slug of water from her tepid tin canteen. "Are you still intent on getting guns at El Mirador?" She shot him a sideways glance as she spoke.

He didn't answer at first but then shook his head. "I will help you first. If that doesn't work, we move onto my plan. Getting guns and going to the ranches."

"Sounds good. I can fire a weapon."

"You will wait at Uaxactun. Take in the sights. See a few ruins, maybe?"

"Take in the sights?" Gabriella felt her face grow red. "I'm probably just as good a shot as you. I didn't come halfway across the world to look at ruins. I came here to find my husband." She had stood and was pacing.

"My apologies. You are right. I will not try to protect you. What is your plan?"

Staring at him and his face in the light of the fire, she couldn't see his scar. She fought back a desire to ask him how he got the jagged ripple. Right now, she needed to find Donovan. This man could help her and that was all that mattered.

She settled back onto the stump. "Okay. My plan is to walk the ten-mile radius in a grid pattern. We can split up four ways, or pair up. Either way. It should take all day to do the first portion."

Nico listened and nodded. "Why don't I pair with Cristo and you pair up with Rafael since they are the experts, the guides? That way we won't be two more *gringos* lost in the jungle, eh?"

"That's what I was thinking. With your help, it should only take two days instead of the four I had planned. So, thank you for that." She peered at him under her eyelashes, a little abashed for lashing out at him a few moments before.

"Yes. It is a good plan."

Nico prodded the fire, which was slowly dying. He looked around for more firewood. "I don't think I can go to sleep this early."

"Me, either," Gabriella said. The coffee Rafael had handed her at dinner packed a powerful punch. And the thought of lying in bed for hours under that mosquito netting listening to the sounds of the jungle outside seemed like torture.

Nico searched the parking lot and then disappeared behind a small shed. He came back triumphant, holding two large logs.

He put two of the logs on the burning embers and then stoked and blew them until the flames had risen again, casting orange shadows on their faces.

Gabriella leaned forward warming her hands. "This is nice. Reminds me of going camping on the coast with my uncles when I was a kid."

"I would have liked to have known Gabriella the girl. I bet you were a handful for your parents," He said it with a small teasing laugh.

But Gabriella tensed. He noticed and quickly became sober.

"Was that out of line? I apologize."

"It's not your fault," she said. "I *was* a handful and my childhood was amazing. For the first few years."

Nico looked at her, waiting.

"My sister was kidnapped and killed."

"That is terrible," Nico said. "I'm so sorry."

Gabriella nodded staring at the fire. For a few seconds they both sat there in silence.

"Excuse me. I have a brilliant idea, possibly my best idea yet." Nico stood and headed for the back end of the Range Rover. In a few seconds, he returned with a bottle of cabernet in one hand and two crystal wine glasses.

"I was saving these for Uaxactun, but this is a much better occasion."

When Nico held the bottle out to her, Gabriella recognized the vintage as one out of her price range at the same time the firelight reflected off his watch. A Patek Philippe. The least expensive Patek Philippe watch sold for about ten thousand dollars. The most expensive one for eight hundred thousand dollars. It was like walking around with a luxury car or a five-bedroom home on your wrist.

"I'm surprised you didn't hire a guide with a motorhome," Gabriella said staring at his watch when he sat back down.

He flashed an embarrassed smile and shrugged. "Let's just say that the watch, the car, the clothes … my life hasn't always been like this. So maybe I hold some luxuries too dear. It is a fault of mine, a weakness, or a character defect you might say. I like the finer things in life because for so long I didn't have them."

Handing her a glass of the wine, he leaned forward and stared into the fire, watching the flames lick the black night.

Gabriella thought about his words, shooting sideways glances at his profile cast in an orange glow. He'd mentioned that he had grown up in Southern Italy. The poorest part of the country. Most people who lived there were desperately impoverished. Somehow he had escaped

his poverty. But how? It wasn't as easy as it was in America. She

wondered if it was his job.

"I didn't know the Italian government paid so well." She said it

lightly, but pointedly.

He scoffed. "Ha! I married into money."

Gabriella sat back shocked. He caught her glancing down at his

left hand. There was no ring.

"I'm a widower."

"I'm sorry."

"Don't be. It was a marriage of convenience. I cared for her, of

course, but only as a dear friend. She was much older than I. She

married me so I would always be there to escort her to her charity

events and be by her side in public. You could say I was a trophy

husband. And, naturally, she wanted me for sex."

Naturally. Gabriella burst out laughing. "Well, she obviously

was a smart woman."

As soon as the words left her mouth, she was embarrassed. She

looked down into her wine glass, feeling her cheeks grow warm. Why

did she say that? The wine must be stronger than she realized. Even so,

she took another large gulp to cover her embarrassment and give her

time to recover.

Nico gave a quick glance to the jungle behind them.

"The natives say the jaguars are the least of your worries if you get lost in the jungle."

"Huh?" Gabriella wrinkled her nose.

"Cristo said not to stay up too late because during the witching hour the *sisimite* and the *sihuanaba* come out.

Although, if I had a choice of the two, I'd rather contend with the *sisimite*," Nico said, taking a swig of his wine. "It's a ghoul who lures you into the deep jungle only to steal your ability to speak."

He paused.

"Forever?" Gabriella shot a quick glance into the jungle.

"Apparently. I didn't ask if it was a temporary state or not."

"What's the other one, the sig-something do?" Gabriella reached over and poured herself a second glass of the wine.

"The *sihuanaba* is very sneaky. She usually comes out on nights like tonight—dark, moonless nights. She is usually naked and at first men only see her from behind. From behind she looks like a beautiful woman with long hair and a very shapely body. Sometimes she takes on the appearance of a man's girlfriend or wife. Men can't help themselves and follow her deep into the woods. When the man gets close enough she turns around—she actually has a skull or horse for a face."

"Lovely."

"But you needn't worry as much about her. She only wants men and I think, but I could be wrong, that she usually only wants unfaithful men."

"Really. That is so perfect," Gabriella snickered, feeling the wine hit her hard. "What does she do to them?"

"She either scares them to death or eats their faces."

"Only the unfaithful guys?"

Nico nodded.

"That sounds fine to me."

As she leaned back to get the last of her wine out of her glass, Gabriella felt something large fall on the back of her head, in her hair. Before she could react, Nico leaped from the stump he was sitting on and hit her head with his palm in a scooping motion. Stunned, Gabriella saw a huge tan spider fall onto the ground in front of her.

She jumped back as the spider landed upside down near the fire. It instantly flipped over in what seemed like fury. It's long furry legs extended about six inches out from its body. Nico grabbed a stick and prodded it.

To Gabriella's astonishment, the spider reared up on its hind legs and started scuttling toward Nico and the stick, exposing what looked like a juicy bright red mouth.

Nico calmly pounded the stick down onto the spider. The spider was so big, the blow didn't squish it, just stunned it or killed it.

"Aha. Mama was protecting her babies. She didn't mean to go after you. She was probably just coming down to the ground out of the tree to hunt to feed her babies and accidentally landed in your hair."

Looking up, Gabriella saw she'd been sitting under a small branch that had extended out from a nearby tree. It must have dropped from the branch onto her head. An accident? The spider didn't mean to go after her? Gabriella didn't buy it. Anything that big didn't seem likely to do something "by accident." She couldn't help but think the mama spider was ticked off and wanted to bite her for some reason. It was irrational to think so, but something about being deep in this jungle made her believe it.

Normal things—people, shadows, spiders—took on a surreal cast. She looked back up into the boughs of the trees and shivered, imagining hundreds of little spiders plotting to find her room in the night. Like in Charlotte's Web, but instead of sweet little things, these were malicious killers waiting to pounce.

Using two sticks, Nico scooped the furry limp insect into the fire, making sure to bury it in the ashes. "I was right," he said. "She has a belly full of babies."

Relief filled Gabriella. The babies were right there, not watching her from above with their millions of eyes.

Gabriella, still huddled a few feet away where she had jumped back away from the spider, watched with wide eyes as the flames licked at the spider's body.

"What the fuck was that?" she finally said.

Nico chuckled. "That beauty was the famous Brazilian Wandering Spider. The deadliest spider in this jungle. Something I had hoped to avoid during our travels here."

"It could eat a mouse."

"Yes, it could."

"What would have happened if it had bit me?"

Nico's eyes narrowed. "Maybe you would have died. It is the most venomous spider I know. And we are deep in the jungle. At the very least, if you were exceedingly lucky, you would have been extremely ill for a long time."

Gabriella tried to brush off her revulsion and the shiver that ran down her back at his words. Normally she wasn't afraid of spiders. But the biggest one she'd seen in San Francisco in her entire life had been an inch long. Not five inches long. And the spiders in the Bay Area didn't rear back on their hind legs and attack you when you thwarted their bite.

Swallowing she looked down around her feet in case there were more. Maybe the babies' daddy or something was coming to seek revenge for the mama's death.

When she looked up, Nico's face was right in front of her. His mouth sought hers. It was warm and tantalizing. Her body betrayed her and reacted, hungrily matching his urgency. Soon every part of her body was pressed against his.

But then realization struck and she drew back. She pushed her hands on his shoulders and moved him away. "I'm married."

She stood and turned away. Her reaction, her ready response, must have been due to the adrenaline rush from seeing the spider. He came up behind her and kissed her neck. "Donovan is dead, Gabriella. It's time you face that."

In one smooth motion, she pushed him away and turned around, eyes wild with fury.

"Don't ever say my husband's name again." She gritted the words out.

"I'm sorry." Nico looked chastened and took a step toward her. If he came a step closer, she was going to push him, Gabriella thought. But he stopped a foot away. "But I'm not sorry for kissing you. It is clear that you desire me as I desire you. It is natural. Normal."

"I don't want you that way," Gabriella said, knowing that her lie was obvious to both of them. "I want your help in finding my husband. That is the only thing I want from you."

"I respect that. Although you cannot deny the chemistry between us, I accept that it is obviously not to be."

He leaned over and before she could back away, he kissed her lightly on the forehead. "I will see you in the morning."

CHAPTER FOURTEEN

Lying in her bed under the mosquito net, Gabriella tried to take her mind off all the spiders she imagined surrounded her bed. Ever since she'd run into Nico, things had taken a surreal bent. She didn't feel like herself at all. Her life back in San Francisco seemed like a dream. All that seemed real was what she could feel and touch right before her in the middle of the jungle.

It was hard to ignore where she was. The night sounds of the jungle seemed mere inches away. Upon closer inspection when she had returned to her room, she glanced at the screen window closing off one wall from the jungle. It didn't have a chance in hell of stopping something that truly wanted to get in her room. Besides parrots and monkeys and jaguars and tapirs, she wasn't sure what else was out there. She couldn't help but feel an ominous presence right outside, not far from where the tree line began.

Was the *sisimite* or the *sihuanaba* out there somewhere watching her and waiting?

To think that millionaires paid a fortune to sleep in this room seemed insanity to her right at that moment.

For the first time, Gabriella questioned coming to Guatemala. It wasn't Disneyland. It wasn't Cancun. This was about as far removed from her regular life as she could be. Had Donovan felt the same way on his many trips away from home? Did he, like she did, feel so incredibly distant from her real life, that it began to feel that her life in San Francisco was something she had dreamed? Did he feel this disconnect that made kissing another person not only feel wonderful, but right?

At the same time, her brief kiss with Nico felt like an enormous betrayal. She had to admit she'd been attracted to him back when she saw him at Lake Josephine before Donovan's plane crash. Something about his scar and sensuous mouth. How did widows ever fall in love and marry again, especially ones who did so soon after a loved one had died?

She could see how under the right circumstances, spouses who traveled the majority of time for their jobs could easily stray. She'd never been jealous of the women Donovan worked with, but now she started to question everything she had once taken for granted.

Now that she had shared a kiss with another man for the first time in years, she understood. If Donovan had strayed, she already forgave him. If, one day she learned that on one of his many trips, he had grown lonely and succumbed to another woman, it would break her heart, but she would forgive him. He would probably be harder on himself than she was about it, trying to live with that guilt.

Thinking back, Gabriella remembered their last moments together, the last time they made love. No, he had never strayed. She would know. He was the type of man who wouldn't be able to live with himself if he had betrayed her.

Could she live with herself for betraying his memory? The wedding vows said until death do us part, but without a body did that still hold true? Without proof positive how could she even consider being with another man? That was yet another reason this trip she was on was so crucial. She would never move on until she had done everything in her power to find Donovan's remains.

Here, deep in the jungle, she felt like a whole new and different person. She wasn't Gabriella the reporter. Or an Italian-American Catholic woman. Or Grace's mama. Or "Ella" —Donovan's wife. Here she was just Gabriella.

The fragility of life was apparent every second in this country. When a large tree blocked their Jeep, they were helpless to do anything on their own. This was a country where you depended on others. She was in a wild land with dangerous terrain and perils, such as poisonous snakes and spiders, wild animals and drug lords who would just as soon kill you as say hello. For the first time, she wondered if she had risked her life to come here. Had she risked making Grace an orphan?

But it was too late to turn back.

As she drifted off to sleep, her body betrayed her again. Nico's hot mouth was on her own and his hard body pressed against hers, she jolted awake, flushed with desire and guilt. It had been months since a man had touched her. That explained why one kiss was driving her mad. Her body yearned to be touched and stroked and pleasured.

So, she laid back and instead imagined Donovan's face and body as she caressed herself. But his image was hazy and vague and his features kept fading in and out.

The same thing had happened with his scent two months ago. For the first month he was gone, she could instantly recall his scent. Even when it had faded from his pillow and clothes, she could recall it in her memory so vividly, it came back to her and she could really smell him. The first time this happened, she was astonished, as if his ghost was in the room with her. She did some research on olfactory recall and found it was true. You could remember a scent so vividly that your nose thought it smelled it again.

Now, lying in her jungle bed, with the screeching of monkeys and birds and God knows, maybe jaguars, all around her, she tried with all her heart to bring Donovan's face into focus before her closed eyelids.

Sometimes she'd be so close. She'd get a glimpse of his eyes as clear as day, but then the rest of his features would fade. She'd focus on the memory of his mouth, but then when her imagination moved up to his cheekbones and eyes, she'd see Nico's ice blue eyes with thick black lashes.

Goddamn it.

She sat up, all lust fading, replaced by her grief and frustration. She couldn't even remember what her husband's face looked like. It was another cruel blow she hadn't expected. She curled up, weeping, hugging herself, her stomach cramped in pain from her grief.

Finally, she fell into a deep heavy sleep, exhausted from crying.

CHAPTER FIFTEEN

"Do not move an inch."

The voice in her ear was low and deadly.

A scratchy palm held her forehead down on the pillow, pressing down hard. Another hand was on her chest, also pushing her into the mattress. And yet another hand that smelled of dirt and sweat was clasped over her mouth. At least two people. And something cold at her throat. She slowly opened her eyes. Beyond a flashlight beam, she could make out the silhouettes of at least three heads hovering over her bed.

One leaned down close to her ear for a second time.

"Don't move or the blade will slice your throat. Do you understand? Blink once if you do."

Fear shot through her body making her want to jump up and run, but she blinked.

"I'm going to take my hand off your mouth. You scream. Blade cuts. Blink if you understand."

Gabriella blinked once, slowly and deliberately.

"Good. I take my hand away now." He spoke in a whisper still as he moved away from her head.

She couldn't make out features on any of the faces, blinded by the flashlight beam.

"Now, you get up and get dressed. If you try to run or scream, we cut you. And then we must also kill Concetta and Manuel so they do not tell who killed you."

Gabriella pressed her lips together tightly. They would kill the owners of the hostel if she tried to fight.

"If you do as we say, they sleep right through and we will let them be. Agree? You can nod."

Gabriella nodded. She would go quietly. The threat to the owners was enough to ensure her silence and cooperation. These men knew that. Throwing her legs over the bed, she stood wearing the tank top and underwear she slept in.

One of the figures tossed her pants, boots, socks, and lightweight jacket on the bed.

She tugged on her clothes and boots and stood. She began to reach for her sunglasses and baseball cap on the nightstand beside the bed, but looked up waiting for permission until one of the men nodded his ascent.

Tugging the hat on, she tucked her sunglasses into her jacket pocket. She eyed her bags on the ground. One man noticed and sharply shook his head. No.

The man behind her gave her a slight shove.

Outside her room, she tripped on something on the walkway in the dark. It was too dark to see what it was. Someone grabbed her elbow to steady her. When the man did, his flashlight skittered across the floor and Gabriella gasped. The man clasped his hand across her mouth to stifle her scream. Rafael lay propped up near her door in the hall, his throat slit in a red smile, the front of his shirt soaked with blood.

Bile filled Gabriella's mouth. Keep it together. She couldn't fall apart. She had to keep her wits about her. If they wanted her dead, they would have already done so. Something else was going on.

Down the stairs, a man in a ski mask taped her hands behind her and slapped a strip of duct tape across her mouth.

He dragged her toward the parking lot, tugging on her bound wrists to guide her. They passed the remains of their earlier campfire. Cristo's legs were sticking out of the fire pit as if he had dived into it. She couldn't see his torso or head, but when the wind shifted, Gabriella gagged on the smell of burning flesh. Fear shot through her.

Turning her head away she said a silent prayer for the two guides. But again, the fact that she was still alive must mean something. Did they think they could hold her for ransom? Maybe they knew The Saint was her father-in-law. He not only had money, but he had immense power.

Opening up the back doors of the van, the man gestured for Gabriella to step inside the darkness. Some primal fear stopped her short. A putrid smell and general evil emanated from that dark metal encased space. Horrible things had happened inside that van. Gabriella knew it as certainly as she knew her own name. Every cell in her body rebelled against getting any closer. Without giving her another chance to comply, the man grabbed her off the ground by her waist and in one fluid movement threw her inside. Without her arms to brace her fall, she landed heavily on one shoulder and yelped in pain behind the duct tape. As she turned to right herself, she felt another body underneath her. She jerked away but then breathed heavily in relief when she felt the body move.

Someone slammed the doors to the van shut and the vehicle moved with a jolt. Light from the dashboard filtered back to where she lay. Scooting around so she could face the other person she saw it was Nico. His eyes were calm and reassuring above his own strip of Duct tape. Without saying a word, they both maneuvered until they were

sitting up, backs pressed against the van across from each other.

CHAPTER SIXTEEN

They drove through the night. The next morning, they stopped to let her and Nico go to the bathroom on the side of the road, eat some beans and rice and drink some water. The scrabbling sounds on the jungle floor seemed to grow louder as the sun rose.

The kidnappers untied them after the first stop.

"Where are they taking us?" Gabriella ripped off the tape across her mouth.

Nico shrugged and held his finger up to his lips gesturing toward the men in the front seats.

"Why?" She mouthed, emphasizing it with a shrug.

He shook his head.

They sat in silence. She arched her neck to see into the front seat. The man in the passenger seat turned to look at them every once in a while, but didn't seem concerned about them trying to escape.

Two big guns, one on the passenger's lap, were a good deterrent to any attempt at overpowering the men.

At one point, Gabriella crawled to the back of the van to check out the doors. They could only be opened from the outside. With a sigh, she moved back to her seat, closing her eyes and trying to sleep.

Gabriella worried that her mother and Grace would hear about the kidnapping and be frantic. Would the motel owners, if they truly were still alive, report the kidnapping?

Remembering how frail her mother had seemed that day at the pool worried her. What if the news that Gabriella was kidnapped cause a heart attack or stroke? It was hard to accept that Maria was growing old but it was reality. Gabriella wasn't ready to lose her mother. Gabriella wished she had called her mother on the satellite phone when they landed. Rafael had said the batteries were weak and needed to be saved in case of an emergency so she had planned on calling home when they got to Uaxactun.

Now it was too late.

During their next stop, the sun had set and the jungle had grown chilly, so while Gabriella waited for the men to finish doing their business behind the van, she stuck her hands in the pockets of her jacket. The jacket was new, bought specifically for the trip, so it was the first time she'd put her hands in the pockets. Now her fingers closed around what felt like a small envelope with something inside. She pulled it out and in the light from the headlights saw it said, "Gabriella" in her mother's familiar handwriting. Quickly, before the men returned

to bind her hands, she tucked the envelope into a zippered pocket on

her cargo pants where it wouldn't fall out.

During the next stop, at dawn, Gabriella crept deeper into the

woods for privacy. The men didn't say anything to her so she went

even further. After doing her business, she peered through the dense

jungle and couldn't see the men or road or hear them.

She turned and ran.

Branches and leaves slapped against her face as she darted

blindly into the forest. After a few seconds, she heard a shout. She ran

faster. Her boots oozed into deep mud and she realized she was in some

wetlands so she changed course, straining to hear the men chasing her.

Once she was on dry ground again, she paused for a second to catch her

breath and tried to hear the men. She couldn't hear a thing but she knew

they weren't far behind.

She ran toward what seemed to be a brighter patch of jungle.

As she did, she heard an odd sounding whistle and knew it was one of

the men signaling the other. Then, a whistle from the other side. They

were close. They were flanking her and closing in.

Rounding a bend, she saw ice blue water of a river and then a

small waterfall pouring down what almost seemed like large stone

steps.

Now she could hear the men. The river looked too deep to cross and there was a larger waterfall below. She headed toward the small waterfall and carefully scaled the stone steps to the top. There, the water was shallow enough to cross. She splashed her way across and paused on the opposite shore, looking down at where she had come from. The two men, holding their guns in front of them, stood on the banks of the river looking downstream. She ducked into the forest, hoping they didn't see her.

Continuing to head upstream on an animal path that seemed to flank the river, Gabriella ran until her face was bloody with scratches and her sides ached.

Then she saw something that made her freeze.

Ahead, was a small stone ruin rising from the jungle, covered in ivy and overgrown plants. It was only eight feet tall.

It was the top of a ruin sticking out of a hillside that had formed around it. As soon as she got to the ruin, something in the atmosphere seemed off, as if the pressure had increased. Her skin prickled with fear. Was someone watching her? It felt like somebody was there but she turned in a circle, squinting into the dark jungle around her, seeing nothing.

But the ominous feeling wouldn't leave. She felt disoriented, as if she had lost her sense of direction. She peered into the fronds of leaves. Had she come from that direction? She whirled and looked to the other side. Or had she come from there? Think. She couldn't flee the way she had come or she'd smack right into the two men chasing her. She listened for any sound that the men were close but didn't hear anything. That's when she realized what was off, what was wrong.

Here in this small clearing with the ruin, the jungle animals had grown deathly silent. The familiar cacophony of scrabbling creatures on the jungle floor, the singing and cawing of birds in the canopy above, and the other deeper animal noises had all ceased as soon as she set foot in the clearing.

Across the clearing, twenty feet away, off to one side of the jumble of ruins, she saw something in the bushes that looked like a person. Stepping out of the bright sunlight and into the shadows of the clearing had probably affected her eyesight. She squinted until her eyes adjusted but she didn't see any movement. Still, there was a pale round spot in the middle of some greenery, almost like a face peering out at her. She took a step closer, eyes narrowed, trying to focus on the whitish round circle that was some five feet above the ground. She took another step and saw it *was* a face. A ghoulish, skeletal face. She gasped. As she did, the face disappeared, greenery closing around where it had once been.

The faintest clicking noise to one side sent terror spurting through her. She whirled in fear, expecting to see something standing on the top of the ruin, watching her, but there was nobody and nothing there.

When she turned back, she nearly screamed. The two gunmen stood at the edge of the clearing watching her. Not saying a word.

One man gestured with his head that she should come their way.

She shook her head slowly.

The other man lifted his gun and beckoned with his other hand for her to come their way. She narrowed her eyes, confused.

The two gunmen were not talking. They also were not entering the clearing.

One of them shot a look at the other and she realized they were terrified. Petrified of something in the clearing and unwilling to enter it.

For a second, she wrote it off to superstitious natives, but then such an icy cold chill ran down her back that she nearly screamed. Instead she swallowed back her fear.

Something wasn't right here. Some primordial evil lived here. She knew it just like she knew there was a sun in the sky.

Making the sign of the cross, she closed her eyes for a second. When she opened them, all she saw were the two men. Both had leveled their guns at her threateningly. One put his hand on the trigger. Even from across the small clearing, she could see sweat drip down his cheek. It wasn't from the heat.

He gave her a look, a warning.

She nodded and headed their way. As soon as she reached the edge of the clearing, one man grabbed her jacket and yanked her deeper into the woods. They pushed her until the clearing was nearly twenty feet behind them, just a bright spot in the dark jungle. They stopped and one man slapped a strip of tape back on her mouth, yanked her hands behind her back and cinched them together. All the while, she watched the other man, who kept darting nervous glances back at the clearing, biting his lip, sweat still pouring down his temples.

CHAPTER SEVENTEEN

When they got back to the road, the kidnappers flung open the door and shoved her into the back of the van, where Gabriella landed with a thud.

One of the men climbed in the back and Nico got the same treatment minus the tape over his mouth.

He raised his eyebrow and she shrugged.

"You okay?" he asked.

She nodded and then curled up into a ball to sleep, exhausted from her escape attempt.

Gabriella drifted off into a nightmare-laden sleep that took place at the ruins in the clearing. No matter how often she turned around, and she whirled in circles, until she was dizzy, she could never catch sight of the evil entity that was always just behind her.

That night, when they stopped to let her use the bathroom and eat, Gabriella stuck close to the road, not caring if the three men saw her going about her business. She was relieved when it was time to crawl back into the van.

On the morning of the second day, while the barest hint of sunrise was pinking the sky above, the two men in the front seat became livelier, chatting in Spanish. Gabriella, who had tried to sleep most of the time, sat up, raising her eyebrows at Nico. She could only make out a few words. *El jefe*. The boss. *Hacienda*. Estate. *Drogas*. Drugs. *Envio*.

Envio? She didn't recognize that word, she shrugged at Nico.

"Shipment," he whispered.

And then the men talked about their plans for the weekend involving beer, women, and dancing. *Cerveza, muchas mujeres*, and *bailando*.

Of course, she was mostly interested in the first part of the conversation about *el jefe, hacienda, and drogas. Envio*.

Obviously they were in the hands of someone working for the Cartel.

The only reason she could fathom was that they were after a ransom. She was sure that in many drug-ruled countries in Central America, kidnapping wealthy American citizens must seem like a lucrative business.

A bit later, as the road seemed to smooth out and became less bumpy, Nico listened to the men's conversation and nodded, leaning over to whisper to her. "We are almost to our destination, wherever that might be."

From what little Gabriella could see out the front windshield and two back windows, they were still deep in the rainforest. After a while, the van slowed and made a sharp turn onto a smaller road. About one hundred feet in, hidden from the main road, was a tall gate flanked by jungle too thick to drive through or around. On the other side of the gate was a paved road. As they approached, the gate swung open automatically. After they passed through, Gabriella turned and saw it slide closed behind them.

The van continued to climb the small mountain. At one point, the driver swerved to a stop and gestured for Gabriella and Nico to look out the front windshield. A huge jaguar was lolled on the side of the road, its eyes glowing yellow in the pre-dawn dark. The driver honked and it lazily stretched and headed off into the surrounding jungle. The passenger turned and said something in Spanish to Nico. Gabriella understood enough to realize that the surrounding fenced land had been stocked with the large jungle cats and smaller prey to feed them.

After another five miles the sun had risen and they'd reached the summit of the hill where there was a twelve-foot-high stone wall with barbed wire on top and another gate blocking their path. The gate swung open as they got closer. Once they were through it, they summited a small hill, a huge, three-story hacienda with a red-tile roof

came into view. The hacienda was perched on a large flat plateau at the

top of the mountain. It reminded Gabriella a bit of Hearst Castle except

instead of zebra and other wildlife roaming the grounds the owner had

jaguars.

They pulled into a huge circle drive. The house was an

enormous three-story stucco palace encircled by a huge, shady veranda

stocked with chaise lounges and tables and chairs.

Outside the van, the gunmen untied her wrists, ripped the tape

off her mouth, and gestured that she should follow them inside.

Inside the house was filled with expensive furniture, leather

and velvet chairs and chandeliers and gigantic art pieces. Gabriella

recognized a Joan Miro and a Picasso as she was whisked through a

large dining room and down a hall.

They stopped in the open doorway of a giant bedroom with a

large bed, fireplace, and long windows overlooking the veranda. She

stalled in the doorway watching as they led Nico to another room just

down the hall. Although his back was to her, he gave her a thumbs up

behind his head. For some reason, that small gesture made Gabriella's

shoulders relax. It was going to be okay. At least for now.

A small, fine-boned woman led Gabriella into a bedroom,

pointing to the bed and the closet. The woman wore an apron and there

was a silver streak in the black hair she had neatly tucked in a bun.
Gabriella followed her into a large closet.

The woman held out a silky nightgown, thrust it at Gabriella
and pointed at the bed.

Gabriella understood. She was supposed to take a nap now.

"*La cena es a las siete.*" Dinner was at seven. Now the woman
took a slinky red dress off the clothes rack and held it up against
Gabriella. And she was supposed to dress for it.

Gabriella nodded. The woman smiled and then left the room.

Fingering the dress and nightgown, Gabriella realized
something with a start. They were her size. Size eight. Quickly, her
blood racing, she flipped through the hanging clothes and then stooped
down and examined the dozen shoes, high heels, flat sandals, and
boots. Her face turned numb. They were her size. Size seven.

It couldn't be a coincidence. The shoes and clothes still had
price tags on them. They hadn't belonged to some other woman in this
house who just happened to wear the same size clothing and shoes.
This had been planned.

She threw the designer clothing down on the floor and
stripping off her cargo pants, curled up under the soft bed covers in her
underwear and tank top. She didn't want to sleep. She wanted to
explore the room and see ways to escape but she could barely keep her

eyelids open. Sleeping in the van had been next to impossible. A good few hours of sleep would make her sharp and rested to plan her escape that night.

Six hours later, Gabriella woke up. Yawning, she looked at the clock. It was 5:45. Someone was knocking on her door. "One minute please."

Before opening the door, she threw on her grimy black cargo pants, kicking the silky red dress into a corner as she walked by it. In the small bathroom, she found some facial cleanser, a toothbrush and toothpaste, so she washed her face, brushed her teeth and ran her fingers through her messy hair.

These bandits might be keeping her against her will but she wasn't going to do as they pleased. Opening her door, Gabriella paused before she took her first step into the hall. She had a feeling she was going to meet her captor.

The woman with the apron was waiting. She gestured for Gabriella to follow her. She glanced at Gabriella's clothes with a worried look but didn't say anything.

Passing by several doors to giant rooms, the woman led Gabriella to an outside door. As they rounded a corner, she saw Nico standing before a man seated at a small iron table. To the right of the table another man stood ramrod straight with his hands clasped behind his back. He wore a white linen suit and dark sunglasses that hid his

eyes. His hair was cut close and he had a neatly trimmed beard and

goatee.

"*El Loro*," the woman murmured.

When she got close, Gabriella saw the man called *El Loro* was

wearing a Carnival-style mask with a long birdlike nose and brilliant

green, turquoise, and yellow feathers, like a parrot. He wore a black

cape and black, knee-high boots.

The woman in the apron gestured that she should stand next to

Nico who was about ten feet away from the man at the table.

Gabriella wondered how long it would take her to grab the

man's gun, an old-looking revolver, off the table in front of him.

The table was covered in a tile mosaic picture of the Virgin de

Guadalupe. The man was poking at a pomegranate, plucking its seeds

and putting them in a small glass bowl, his fingers dripping with the red

juice onto the table. His hands, the only part of his skin that showed,

were startling white. The man in the white suit behind him didn't

appear to have a gun, but who knew.

"You shall both be treated as my guests," the masked man said,

not looking away from the pomegranate. "You will have the run of

most of the first floor of the hacienda. The second and third floors are

my own private quarters so they are off limits. But please make yourself comfortable in the other portions of the first floor. In addition to your private rooms, the first floor features a library, a fine dining room and the kitchen.

"Esmeralda, my esteemed chef and housekeeper, will fix your meals and answer any questions you might have. I can't imagine it happening after you eat Esmeralda's cooking but if you find you need to snack, please help yourself to any food in the kitchen. You are my guests. If you act like a guest, you will come to no harm."

The man wiped the reddish pink juices from his fingers onto a pale pink silk cloth, staining it with droplets of red.

They would have access to *most* of the rooms on the first floor, Gabriella thought, scrunching her face. What were in the other ones?

"Yes, *senor*," Nico said in a low voice beside her.

Gabriella stayed silent glaring at the man. She would not speak until he looked at her. The man ignored her, continuing to concentrate on the fruit in front of him.

"You will find your stay here to your liking, I'm certain. It is one of my finest homes. I will leave you here while I am on business. My assistant, Marco, will be here more often than I am and he will also be answer any questions you might have that Esmeralda doesn't have answers to."

The man in the white suit gave a slight nod.

The masked man continued prodding the pomegranate, sticking one beefy white finger inside the fruit up to a knuckle before extracting a seed between a finger and thumb. Holding the tiny seed, he held it up to his mask, examined it and then delicately stuck the seed through a small mouth hole, leaving red stains along the edges of the opening.

Finally, he looked up.

"Why am I here?" Gabriella gritted the words.

The man gave the slightest shrug. "I don't think that is necessary for you to know that at this time."

"Who are you?"

"Some call me *El Loro*."

"Let me at least call my mother. She must be worried sick." Inside, Gabriella was more worried about Grace, but didn't want this man to hear her daughter's name or that she even had a child.

"Ms. Giovanni. Your mother and daughter have been told that you were killed in a kidnapping attempt gone awry. They will not miss you."

Gabriella practically fell to her knees, imagining Grace's face on hearing the news. For a few seconds, she saw black. It was only Nico's grip on her elbow that kept her from collapsing.

The man gave a loud sigh. "Yes, I'm sorry to cause them that type of pain. But this will prevent anyone from looking for you, which would be inconvenient for us."

Us.

"Fuck you." Gabriella said the words in a low growl. She shot a glance at the man in the white suit. He hadn't moved.

The man chuckled. "Not so fast. You should still be polite to me. You see, if you behave, enjoy yourself, and are not a problem to my staff, or me, there is still a chance you will be able to return to your mother and daughter. And just think how happy they will be to see you rise from the dead, so to speak. It will be a miracle."

Gabriella steeled herself. She needed to be smart. She needed answers.

"What must happen for me to return home?"

"Alas, that is not something I can discuss with you."

Frustration filled her.

"What can I do to hasten that return?"

"Aha. I know you feel helpless so let me reassure you there is nothing you *can* do to speed up your possible return. But there are things you can do to prevent it. If you act like a guest here and do not cause any problems, you will have no potential conflicts that will prevent your homecoming."

He pushed back the chair and stood. He was at least six feet tall, which was unusual in this country.

"Enjoy your stay. Esmeralda has prepared a dinner to die for. I'm very sad that another appointment awaits me and I will miss her cooking. She is the finest chef in Guatemala, which of course is why she is in my employ."

Before Gabriella could say or do anything else, the man had scooped up his gun and shouldered past, the hem of his cape brushing against her bare arm. A second later, the man in the white suit followed.

CHAPTER EIGHTEEN

Sean Donovan stared at the photograph that was becoming slightly soft from his handling. He'd been staring at it for a few weeks and it still didn't mean anything.

Monica's bare breasts pressed against his naked back, making him moan. "Do you recognize her yet?" she asked in her sultry Spanish accent.

He flipped and in one smooth motion her nude body was on top of his on the thin cotton mat and his mouth was on hers. After a few minutes he came up for air.

Finally, he answered her question. "No."

He turned his head to the side squinting at the dim light seeping through the block glass windows near the ceiling. Months ago, when he was first put into his basement prison, Donovan had run his fingers over every inch of the concrete wall. The room was about twelve by twelve feet. He'd counted it out during one of his first days of captivity. Not for any real reason, just for something to do.

The basement's hard clay floors were surprisingly clean. In one corner near the window and wall but not up against it, was his bed— basically a futon mattress on the ground. A small wood table that only reached his knees held a small bowl and cup and pitcher. In the opposite corner, there was a shower stall in the corner without sides or curtains, open to the rest of the basement. A small toilet and tiny sink were next to the shower. Near the toilet was a small metal bucket.

Donovan wasn't sure what it was for. He sometimes used it to stand on to see out the glass block windows. The only thing he could see through the thick glass was a swash of green. Once when he'd heard voices outside, he stood on the metal bucket and saw darker figures moving past, but the rest of the time, he saw moving green images—some type of foliage that sometimes moved with the wind, he figured.

The glass block windows were too small for him to fit through even if he managed to break them.

The dark-haired woman beside him sighed. "You sure? You do not know her?"

Donovan shook his head in frustration.

The woman in the photograph plucked at something deep inside him, but he couldn't have said why or who she was. They kept asking her name. He didn't even know his own name. But he knew somehow the picture was important. Every day, they sent Monica down into the damp dim room to ask him the same question: "Do you recognize her?"

He'd stare at the woman. Her tousled brown hair, dimples, and huge expressive eyes did not trigger any name or memory. She was beautiful. But she meant nothing to him.

Every day it was the same. His captors were so adamant, he wondered if the woman in the photo was a spy they were trying to identify. He knew she looked familiar and something told him to protect her identity, but it didn't matter because he couldn't remember who she was or her name anyway.

His memories only went back a few months. They told him he had hit his head in a plane crash. He remembered waking up in the deep jungle. The men who grabbed him and brought him to this house told him he was an American spy who had important information they needed. They said they were going to keep him in this basement prison until he remembered whom he was and what that information was.

At first, they didn't believe he had truly forgotten and he had long scars on his back to prove it, but then a small, bespectacled doctor had come and examined him, asking him questions while he was connected to a lie-detector machine. That's when they believed he was telling the truth about his amnesia.

Starting on the first day of his captivity, they sent Monica down every day to bring him simple meals of beans and cheese and tortillas. At first, she also bathed him in the tub in the corner until he was able to do it himself. She was gentle in treating the wounds from his beatings. And always, she asked him questions.

When she looked at him, brushing her sleek black hair back from her huge dark eyes and pursing her lips together, Donovan wanted to tell her everything he had ever known and then some. But his mind remained a blank white space.

On about his tenth day of his captivity, when Monica came down, she took off her shirt and gently guided his mouth to her breasts. He didn't object.

Now, some months later, he dreamed of Monica's voluptuous body every night, all night long, tossing and turning with lust until she arrived with the dawn. It was the only thing he had to look forward to in this prison. It was the only thing that kept him from sinking completely into his despair.

This morning she gently took his face in her soft hands and turned him away from the window, back to her. Her mouth pressed on the corner of his and then her tongue trailed his jaw, down his neck, chest and settled on his hip bones until he was groaning in pleasure and straining to get his pants off.

CHAPTER NINETEEN

Back in her room, Gabriella curled up in a ball on the bed. While some tears slipped out of her eyes, more than anything she was angry.

The woman had told her to dress for dinner. Never. They might be able to keep her prisoner here, but she would never do what they want. She'd wear her own clothes until they turned into rags and fell off before she'd wear clothes the man in the mask had picked out for her *in her size.*

Thinking of her own clothes made her remember the envelope with her mother's words on it she had found in her jacket. Quickly, she reached down and retrieved it from the zippered pocket in her pants. Seeing her mother's words would be painful but would motivate her to find a way to escape.

She slit the envelope with a fingernail and took out the pages with her mother's neat handwriting.

Gabriella,

I need to tell you something that is going to be difficult for you to hear.

Please forgive me for not telling you earlier, but I didn't want you to suffer needlessly. And please forgive me for not telling you before your trip, but I didn't want you to change your plans.

I have cancer. A very slow growing cancer, but one that has progressed beyond any type of cure. We first found out six months ago and after many conversations with Vincenzo and lots of prayer, I decided not to seek treatment. It was too far progressed. Even under the best circumstances, I still don't have long to live. I did not want to spend the last few weeks, months, or year of my life sick from the chemotherapy. Instead, Vincenzo and I decided to live each moment that was left to the fullest.

I know you, and I know you will be angry for not telling you before you left. But I know you needed to do this. And I could not ask you to wait until I was gone. I don't know how long I have left. A week? A month? Six months? It wouldn't be fair to you to have to wait.

Instead, we came up with a plan. If it looks like things are growing worse, Vincenzo will send a private jet to Central America to find you and bring you home. The jet is in standby at the airport right now.

This is all I could do. Please understand and respect why I have made the decisions I have made in all this. They weren't easy choices, but were made after much thought and prayer.

Do know that I love you more than the universe and that will never change no matter where my physical body is. My love transcends the physical.

And know that I'm okay with the idea of death. I will be with Caterina and your father and that knowledge fills me with peace. The only regret I have is the sorrow I will leave behind. I don't want you or your brothers to grieve for me. That is what breaks my heart right now. Please try to remember this during the hard times. Please be strong for me. You're a Giovanni. You are strong. Be strong for Grace. She needs you now more than ever. I will be here when you get home and we will talk more.

By the time Gabriella was done reading, the note was crumpled from her grip. Now, with hindsight, she saw how her mother's health had been failing. Now, she understood why The Saint had "retired" six months ago. He wasn't spending the rest of his life making Maria happy; he was going to spend the rest of *her* life making her happy.

Instead of weeping and wailing, Gabriella was numb and stunned. Staring at the wall, she felt something welling up inside her. Out of that numbness came a fierce determination to escape.

She needed a plan.

#

The dining room had long red velvet drapes lining the walls. On one wall, they parted to reveal a floor to ceiling window that opened up to the veranda with the pool's icy blue water sparkling in the background. A cool breeze sucked the drapes in and out like a breath. As darkness fell, tiny lights lining the roof and floor of the veranda turned on. A string of larger lights strung up on old-fashioned lampposts surrounded the paved area bordering the pool.

The dinner so far had taken two hours. The first course, a small shrimp cocktail and champagne was served at seven and then the main course, a massive pan of paella didn't arrive until about seven thirty, accompanied by a bottle of white wine.

Just as the main course was served, the pulsing sound of a helicopter that sounded as if it were right outside the window startled Gabriella. Esmeralda didn't blink and continued ladling out fresh shrimp and scallops saturated in saffron.

Part of Gabriella's plan was to do what the masked man said— not be difficult and enjoy her stay so she could be returned home sooner rather than later. On the surface, at least. Behind the scenes, she would do everything she could to make an escape plan and get back to her mother. So, when nobody mentioned the helicopter, Gabriella pretended to take it in stride. It was the first stage of her temporary acting career.

But as soon as the older woman went back through the swinging doors to the kitchen, Nico leaned over and whispered, "There is a helipad on the roof. I think this is how the man of the house comes and goes."

The man of the house. Who the hell was he? Was he Guatemalan? Gabriella had heard an accent, so English was his second language. He had fair skin rare in these parts.

He used some clichés and colloquialisms that made her think at the very least he had lived in America or been educated there. For instance, using the phrase, "to die for" which was ominous under the circumstances, but also a very American figure of speech.

Whenever Esmeralda was in earshot, she and Nico talked about lighthearted subjects, such as art, film, and books. Gabriella was surprised at how easy it was to talk to Nico. This time, unlike their conversation at the campfire, they avoided anything too personal.

Gabriella raved about the latest mystery she had read, "The Saints of the Lost and Found," and said it had inspired her to take a trip to Louisiana the week after she read it, hoping to relive the scenes in the book, at least in her imagination.

Nico talked about the first time he saw the movie "The Dreamers" and how he fell in love with Eva Green and wanted to quit university and move to Paris.

During a pause in the conversation, Gabriella quelled the urge to ask about his scar. For some reason, maybe because she found it so sexy, bringing it up seemed like an intimacy she wasn't ready to enter with him. She focused on keeping the conversation light. The only urgency was whenever Esmeralda left the room.

That's when they talked about the hacienda and their captor. During the long pauses when Esmeralda was in the kitchen, Gabriella would lean toward Nico and whisper.

"What can you see from your room? Do you think we could escape? How could we get through those gates to the main road? He said we have free reign of the property, let's go outside tonight and figure out our escape plan."

Nico listened carefully and answered each question patiently.

Ultimately, he told her they would probably have to do a little more reconnaissance if they wanted an effective escape plan.

"Right now, we know so little. What I do know is there is a twelve-foot wall surrounding this compound and on the other side, are dangerous animals that probably wouldn't mind a taste of human flesh," he said.

By eight, after the main course was cleared, Esmeralda brought a salad of lightly dressed fresh greens.

"It's very Mediterranean, isn't it?" Gabriella said to Nico.

His brow furrowed and he waited for Esmeralda to return to the kitchen before he answered. "I suspect our host isn't Guatemalan. He seems Spanish. The only thing that makes me wonder is why we are eating so early if he is truly from Spain. Dinner there is more common, at say, ten at night."

"Maybe he is accommodating my American taste?"

Nico nodded, taking a sip of his wine.

By nine, Esmeralda had brought small dishes of dessert—flan drizzled in a fresh caramel sauce—with small goblets of Sangria.

When they finished dessert, Gabriella stood and whipped out some high school Spanish. "*Dónde está el baño?*" Where is the bathroom?

Nico raised an eyebrow and Gabriella winked at him behind Esmeralda's back as she followed the woman into the hall.

A small silver and gold decorated bathroom was off the dining room. Gabriella smiled gratefully and then, while it was true she needed to use the restroom, she waited for several moments until she heard the sound of the woman's footsteps leading away.

Waiting another few minutes, she pressed her ear to the door and then gently opened it. The hallway was empty. Quickly, she raced to the first door, turning the handle. Locked. The next one was locked, as well. Finally, a door opened. But to Gabriella's disappointment it was her own bedroom. There were only three doors left. All were locked but one. Flinging the door open, she realized it was the room they had led Nico to the night before. Standing in the doorway, she caught a whiff of his cologne. His bed was neatly made and a robe was spread over the foot of it. Hearing a noise, she quickly shut the door and turned. Esmeralda appeared out of a doorway at the other end.

"Oh, there you are! I was turned around," Gabriella said.

Settled back in her chair, she waited for Esmeralda to leave before she leaned over to Nico. "Every door was locked except our bedrooms."

Nico nodded. "I could have spared you the trouble. The door on the left-hand side at the end of the hall leads to the second and third stories. If you go out the main door of the dining room behind you, you can access the library and the study. Other than that, everything else is off-limits, as he mentioned earlier."

Gabriella was irritated by Nico's matter-of-fact summary and also because he'd beat her in scouting out the locked door situation.

She quickly got over her irritation when Nico started telling her a funny story about getting caught with his friends skinny-dipping as teenagers. The police officer who ended up shining the light on him and his friends in a neighbor's pool was his girlfriend's father. Needless to say, he never was allowed on another date with the girl again.

After she'd scraped the last bit of flan out of the custard dish, Gabriella was surprised to feel a flicker of disappointment when Esmeralda came to clear the dishes.

Nico stood and held Gabriella's chair so she could stand. When she did, a wave of dizziness struck and she had to grip the edge of the table. All the alcohol, even sipped slowly over a few hours, had apparently added up.

Steading her with his hand on her arm, Nico asked if she were okay.

"I stood up too fast. I should go to bed now." She hoped she wasn't slurring her words.

Nico, one hand placed gently on her back, guider her back to her room. "Are you going to be okay?" he asked as they walked down the hallway.

"I think so. I'll drink a big glass of water and sleep in."

At her door, he gave her a gentle kiss on her forehead and then headed to his own room, a few doors down. She watched, swaying a little on her feet, until he gave her a little wave and entered his room.

CHAPTER TWENTY

Lying on a futon looking up at the ceiling Donovan wondered who he was and why he was here, prisoner in someone's basement.

Monica was propped on one elbow beside him, running her fingernail down his chest, her sleek hair falling in a curtain, staring off into space, caught in her own thoughts.

As he always did after their lovemaking sessions, he peppered Monica with questions. It was their form of pillow talk.

"Why are they keeping me here?"

Monica shrugged.

"Do *you* know who I am?"

She shook her head no to all his questions.

"Will you tell me who is holding me prisoner?"

He asked the same questions every time. She never responded verbally in any way.

Today, for the first time, his increasing frustration led him to turn the questions around and asked about her instead of him and his situation.

"Why are you so loyal to this guy?" He brushed her hand off and sat up, running his fingers through his hair. It felt greasy. He'd wash it today during his shower. He eyed the small shower stall in the corner distastefully. It needed to be cleaned. But it was better than nothing.

Monica opened her mouth to answer and Donovan froze.

"I owe him."

He settled his back against the wall near the futon and tried not to act too eager. She was finally going to tell him something.

"What could you possibly owe him?"

"Everything."

For the next hour, Monica told him her story.

Monica had grown up right in the heart of the Peten jungle. Each morning she and her siblings and mother and father would pack up the baskets to the brim with the small braided bracelets they had woven and travel to the nearest Mayan ruins, at Tikal. There they waited for the daily tour buses to arrive.

They set up shop on a blanket near other vendors of homemade objects such as leather belts, bright ceramic spoon holders and mugs, and hand carved nativity scenes,

When the buses pulled up, a tour guide led the tourists through the ruins, giving the history of the Tikal National Park.

At the end of each tour, the guide, who always received a cut from each vendor set up in the shade of the concrete bathroom stalls, would drop the tourists off to peruse items made by the locals.

Meanwhile, Monica and her three younger sisters ran wild in the surrounding jungle and in between visits from tour buses, played hide and seek in the ruins.

One day, *el jefe*, as Monica called him, pulled up in a giant vehicle, she said. Bigger and longer and taller than anything she'd ever seen. His bodyguards, toting machine guns got out first and cleared the entire area. She later found that he had stopped two tour buses down the road. A gunman watched the terrified tourists, making sure the buses stayed put until *el jefe* was done and gone.

While Monica and her siblings spied from the jungle, a helicopter landed in the middle of a patch of grass between the ruins. A man in a white suit got out. *El jefe* greeted him with a handshake and the men exchanged small packages. They spoke for a few minutes with the helicopter's blades still churning and not long after, the man got back into the helicopter and left. Believing the excitement was over, Monica's siblings ran off to find their mother for lunch. Monica stayed watching until she felt a hand clamp over her mouth. She tried to bite it but the person was too strong and dragged her deep into one of the dark corners of a ruin.

When they were inside, the man let go. It was one of *el jefe's*

gunmen. He ripped off her dress and had his way with her. When she

tried to struggle, he punched her and told her he would kill her entire

family. She didn't struggle anymore She closed her eyes and pretended

she was dead.

She heard the man swear and then grow still on top of her.

When she opened her eyes, *el jefe* was in the doorway, only a dark

silhouette surrounded by streams of light like a vision. Without a word,

he shot the gunman between the eyes.

Pulling her up, *el jefe* straightened out her dress and asked

where her parents were. She told him. Leading her by the hand, he

stood in front of her parents and berated them. Told them that they had

left their daughter unattended and she had been defiled. No man would

ever want her. They should be ashamed and kill themselves right now.

Horrified, Monica had gone to her knees and begged him to

forgive her parents. It was her fault, she said. She should have never

wandered off alone. She was a disobedient child and that is why it had

happened. Even though she knew deep down inside none of it was her

fault, she also knew just as certainly, it wasn't her parent's fault. She

couldn't live with them thinking this was so. She'd rather they scorn

her than blame themselves.

El jefe pulled her up off the ground in front of him. He told her parents he was taking Monica back to live with him. Monica's father turned away so she couldn't see his face, but her mother dropped to her knees this time, begging for him to leave Monica with them

Monica was the one who pulled her mother up and grasped her by the shoulders. Somewhere along the line she had reached her mother's height and then some. Looking her mother right in the eyes, she forced a smile.

"Mama, he killed the man who was hurting me. I owe him my life. I love him. Please let me go and know I will be fine."

Her mother searched her eyes for a long moment and then pressed her lips together tightly nodded. She grasped Monica's hand and pressed something into it. It wasn't until Monica was in the man's large vehicle that she opened her palm and found her mother's tiny silver wedding ring. From that day forward she wore it on a silver chain around her neck.

When they arrived at *el jefe's* hacienda, a maid led Monica to a beautiful room outfitted for a princess, but Monica spent the night in terror with the softest sheets she'd ever felt pulled up to her chin. Every creak of the floorboard, every sound outside her room was *el jefe*, coming to do what his man had done. By morning, despite her trepidation, she could no longer keep her eyes open.

When she awoke, at sunset, a meal was waiting for her on the nightstand: fresh orange juice, sausages, rice, beans, and tortillas. She wept with gratefulness as she ate more food than she'd ever seen in one sitting in her life.

El jefe never came for her and finally Monica relaxed. Occasionally he would call her to his office and ask how she was doing? Soon, she was no longer nervous and told him excitedly about how her English lessons were coming along. He always nodded and then dismissed her. She owed him everything and her loyalty had no end, she told Donovan. That is why she could never answer Donovan's questions.

When she was done, Donovan took her in his arms, kissing her forehead and holding her tight against his chest.

She sat up. "Do you understand now?"

He nodded.

CHAPTER TWENTY-ONE

The next morning, her first one at the hacienda, Gabriella woke full of dread.

And guilt.

Her mother could be dead or dying, her daughter was dealing with losing both her parents within six months and here she was in a drug lord's tropical palace, sleeping in until the sun had warmed the Olympic-sized swimming pool outside. A handsome man flirted with her constantly. She slept under 800-thread count Egyptian cotton sheets, was fed five-course meals by a gourmet chef, and drank $500 bottles of wine.

After a quick shower, Gabriella slipped her cargo pants and tank top back on. She found them—clean and folded—on a chair just inside her bedroom door. Someone had crept into her room during the night, found her wadded up dirty clothes on the floor beside her bed and washed and dried them before she woke.

Creepy.

Slipping out of her room, she crept, barefoot down the hall toward the dining room.

There she found a buffet style breakfast waiting—rolls, fresh fruit and coffee. She heard some noise in the kitchen but nothing else.

Grabbing a roll and mug of coffee, Gabriella headed back into the hall. She skipped the kitchen, but tried every door she passed while keeping an eye out for anyone coming.

The hallway stretched the length of the house and the doors at each end led outside onto the veranda. She exited through the far door and found she was on a shady stretch of porch. She could see the roof of what must be a garage some ways away and beyond that, the twelve-foot stone wall that surrounded the compound. She began walking along the veranda and still didn't see or hear anybody else.

The masked man was right, Gabriella and Nico truly did have free reign of the house and pool.

It was baffling. But when she stood on the long back veranda by the pool and saw the desolate jungle that lay hundreds of feet below the house's hilltop perch, she got some idea why they were not locked up. The hacienda was on top of a hill that overlooked jungle to all sides. The grounds were enclosed by the wall. Last night, the woman had told them the wall was to keep the jaguars out. But it also effectively prevented Gabriella from devising a way to escape. They were miles from anywhere and leaping that fence meant throwing herself into the jungle.

But filled with despair about her mother's decaying health, Gabriella was ready to do just that.

She paced the veranda glancing over her shoulder every few minutes. There didn't appear to be another soul around. She took one step off the veranda and onto the deck of the pool. Circling the pool, she paused on the far side and looked back at the hacienda. It looked sleepy. There was no movement in any of the windows. No faces peeking out watching her. Nobody standing in doorways keeping track of her movements.

Ducking behind a large palm tree, she took a step into the brush below the elevated pool deck. It was further down than she anticipated and she stumbled, having to grab ahold of some branches to stay upright, her ankle twisting painfully.

Looking over at the hacienda, she waited. Nothing. No fluttered curtains or shades. No mad dash outside to stop her.

Turning, she ran toward the stone wall. This portion of it—on the far side of the pool—was the part most heavily hidden by trees and bushes and furthest away from the house.

When she reached the wall, she looked for any place to get a toehold, but the wall was sleek stone.

She noticed a small bucket with a sponge inside. Something the gardeners had left out perhaps. She overturned it and stood, trying to see how much closer to the top of the wall she could get. Not enough. Even stretching her arms, the top was out of her reach.

During her perusal of the veranda, she'd looked for something that could be used as a ladder, but there was nothing.

Now, she eyed a small tree about two feet from the wall. If she scaled the tree to the top, she could reach over and jump to the top of the wall. She grabbed a hold of a piece of bark sticking off the tree a little above her head and then using it to gain leverage, put her right foot on the tree and tried to hoist herself up. Her foot held on the tree trunk, and she grasped the tree with both arms, now about two feet above the ground. Searching the trunk for another piece of loose bark, she found one a few feet above. She reached up. It was too far away. Poking her head around the trunk she examined the other side. There was a piece of bark she could grab. She scooted until she was on the other side of the tree and reached up for the piece of bark starting to come off the trunk. She grabbed it. When she lifted her foot up and her weight was temporarily supported by the bark, it broke off and she fell to the ground, landing on her back with a heavy thud that knocked the wind out of her.

For a few seconds, she couldn't breathe. She struggled to sit up, worried she'd hurt herself.

"Take it easy." The voice was low and amused. "You might have seriously injured yourself."

Now sitting up, she glanced behind her. The sun blocked the man's face, but she recognized his voice. He turned his head and the sun silhouetted his mask with the long-pointed nose. *El Loro.*

"I need to go home. I need to be with my mother. She's dying."

Maybe, if he had half a heart, he would understand this.

Tears of anger and frustration shot out of her eyes. Maybe he would think they were sad tears, but she was furious.

"We've had this discussion already," the man said.

Gabriella shielded her eyes, trying to see him better but he was still just a dark figure with sunlight streaming around him.

"Please."

She would beg if she needed to. The only thing she wanted in the world was to get back to her mother before she died and to be there to comfort her daughter. She would do anything. She stood, relieved to find that nothing hurt except her twisted ankle.

"I'll do anything you want. Anything." She said it with such conviction the man laughed.

"I believe you." He turned his head again. "There is a slight problem."

Gabriella waited.

"There is nothing you have I want."

"If that is true, then let me go. I beg you."

"You serve a purpose. I cannot let you go until something else is resolved. Something that you can do nothing about."

Despair filled Gabriella. She was even more helpless than she realized.

A few other people had arrived. What looked like a gardener, and the cook, Esmeralda and a couple of men dressed in what appeared to be work clothes, matching khaki pants and shirts and boots. She spotted Nico on the pool deck watching. He was near Marco, the man in the white linen suit.

The man stood between her and the pool. The other people stood a little bit away, watching. All of them had blank looks on their faces.

She started walking toward the man in the mask and he held up a palm.

"No. I'm not done."

Gabriella waited. Could she take him? Maybe. But then where would she go and what would she do?

"I obviously did not make myself clear yesterday. If you behave, and this morning's little stunt is not considerate guest behavior—if you behave like a guest, there is a chance you will be able to return to your mother and daughter. You see I am not a monster. I am a businessman. Yes, sometimes my work requires me to act in certain distasteful ways, but it is not my first choice."

Gabriella let out a big breath, thinking he was done.

But then he lowered his voice and leaned forward, so close she could smell the minty toothpaste he had used that day.

"If you try to escape again. I will make sure there is no mother and daughter for you to go home to."

Gabriella's heart stopped for a minute, but he wasn't done.

"That penthouse has some top-notch security, but it is nothing compared to my trained men. They have been inside it already without anyone being the wiser. Your daughter's bedroom is a fine tribute and example of her love of horses and books."

Her head slumped. They had been inside her daughter's bedroom.

"I understand." She didn't look up as she said it. She stared at the ground, watching the largest ants she had ever seen strut across the toe of her boot. She was beaten.

He had won. She was his prisoner and there was nothing she could do about it.

CHAPTER TWENTY-TWO

Gabriella knew who was knocking on her bedroom door even before she threw back the lock. It had become a nightly habit. After "curfew" each night, Nico snuck down the hallway with a small bottle of whiskey and two glasses.

After that day by the stone wall, Gabriella had never seen the man in the mask again or his colleague in the white suit. She'd been at the hacienda for ten days.

Sometimes the desire to escape and find her way—somehow— back to her mother and daughter was nearly irresistible. She'd stand with her hand on the doorknob and close her eyes, willing herself to remain rational.

Meanwhile, her heart would race and she'd become nearly paralyzed by panic attacks.

Thoughts and images of her mother's death haunted her constantly: Maria in excruciating pain, yet protesting the painless peace of death, clinging desperately to life, waiting for The Saint's jet to arrive from Central America with Gabriella so she could say goodbye to her daughter before she slipped into oblivion.

Or worse, Maria willingly taking her last breath, already convinced that Gabriella was dead and she was joining her in the hereafter.

The desperation she felt was overwhelming. Gabriella needed to escape. Of course she was afraid of the man in the mask. He said he'd kill her family. But if she got to a phone, she could stop any threat. *El Loro* was powerful but so was her mother's husband. The Saint wouldn't let anything happen to her mother or daughter if she could only warn him. She needed to be smart about her escape plan. She'd need a vehicle to get away and get to a phone. Or she needed to contact someone to come get her. Those were her only two options.

Although many doors were locked, many were also available to them, including the extensive library the masked man had mentioned. Gabriella had pilfered the library, keeping a big stack of books on her nightstand.

But every time she sat down to read, her frantic thoughts of her mother and Grace would take over.

The only thing that allowed her peace from her thoughts was the nightly visits from Nico when she would drink until her mind shut off and she could tumble into a dreamless sleep.

Because it was her only small measure of peace, it didn't take long before she began to look forward to Nico's nightly visits.

After the first night, Esmeralda told them one other house rule was that they both should be in their rooms each night by ten. It was unclear why that rule was established, but Gabriella had no reason to stay out late anyway. Esmeralda never said they had to each be in their own rooms, so Nico's visits seemed to be approved.

Without his visits, Gabriella would have spent those late-night hours pacing. They sat by her fireplace on the rug, drinking until dawn. She never asked where he got the alcohol.

During his visits, they talked for hours. Gabriella found they had a lot more in common than she initially realized. They both had giant Italian families with characters that were straight out of the movies.

Nico was a surprisingly charming and interesting man. Like that first night over dinner, there was never enough time together to share their thoughts on books, film, and art. They even played chess on an old wooden board he'd brought to her room one night. But it wasn't his first choice since Gabriella usually won fairly fast.

They spent most of their time together sprawled on the rug in front of her bedroom fireplace. Every time he arrived, Nico would start the small blaze for them. The wood in her bin by the fireplace was mysteriously replaced while she was at dinner each night.

Although the talk often veered into lighthearted topics, the main subject was always why they were being held captive.

"I think I know why," Nico would say. "They want me to tell them about my operative who was on the plane. They want … the name."

Gabriella noticed how he changed courses instead of saying "his" or "her" name. He didn't even want her to know if the operative was male or female.

"Just who are they? Sinaloa?" she asked. Sinaloa was known as the most powerful drug cartel in the world. They were also known as the Blood Alliance, the Federation and the Pacific Cartel.

She'd researched them the second Donovan's flight left for Central America months ago. From what she'd found, the Sinaloa Cartel had smuggled nearly two hundred tons of cocaine and heroin into the United States in the past twenty years. Their main arena of operation was in the Mexican states of Sinaloa, Durango, and Chihuahua. That's one reason she was surprised to find that when Donovan's plane went down he was south of Mexico, in Guatemala.

Nico shook his head. *"Los Zetas."*

The name sounded familiar but Gabriella wasn't sure who or what they were.

"*Los Zetas* is a gang of mercenaries. They are all former members of the Gulf Cartel. They were all members of the cartel's special forces. But they got greedy and broke away to form their own cartel. They are the ones smuggling cocaine from Columbia to America."

The Gulf Cartel was the oldest organized crime unit in Mexico. Gabriella knew the defection was not taken lightly.

She shook her head at her naivety, thinking she could tromp through the jungle in Central America to look for her dead husband's body and then waltz right back out again.

"Even our government will not send men here. Your husband was an exception. I've heard rumors that he came here without permission, that he scheduled his own flight down here despite the DEA forbidding him from doing so."

"Good God." Gabriella sat back against the base of the love seat. That revelation explained so much. Of course Donovan would disobey DEA orders if he thought he was on to something larger, bigger, and more relevant.

And that could also mean that the DEA had probably never actually gone to search for him down here. That he'd gone rogue and as punishment, they had cut him loose.

The only question was why the senator had helped her. And how he had received details of Donovan's travels. Maybe under the senator's pressure, the agency had a change of heart. Gabriella found that hard to believe, though.

"If all you say is true," Gabriella began. "Why are they keeping me prisoner? It seems if I were in the way, they would just kill me."

"They think we are lovers?" He let slip a small smile.

"It's not funny."

The word "lovers" made her stomach flip flop.

"I truly think they are using you to get to me," he said. "That is why they let me visit you. Look."

He pointed up to a small Moroccan lamp in one corner of the ceiling. Each corner of her room held a different colored tin lamp. "Those are everywhere. They have cameras inside. Except the bathroom. The senor at least has decency not to pry in that one spot."

"They've been watching us the whole time?" Gabriella felt like she was going to vomit. She was tempted to take a poker from the fire and reach up and try to break the lamps, but she remembered what she had been told by the man in the mask. If she behaved she had a chance of going home to see Grace and spend every precious moment left with her mother.

She'd behave all right. Until he wasn't looking.

Thinking of what the cameras had already witnessed in her room made her skin crawl. Someone had been spying on her and Nico.

Then her fury turned to him. "I don't understand why you didn't say anything sooner." She could almost feel the anger spurting through her veins.

He looked surprised. "I only today realized this. I knocked one over in my room and it shattered. When I was cleaning up the pieces I saw the tiny camera."

Gabriella narrowed her eyes at him. She wasn't convinced he was telling the truth. He might have lied to appease her.

She stood abruptly and headed toward the bathroom. Despite what Nico said about the bathrooms not having cameras, she searched every inch, standing on the counter to search the lights in the ceiling, pulling down every single towel, dumping every drawer.

"You okay in there?" Nico asked.

"Are you sure there isn't a goddamn camera in here, too?" She shouted back.

"I don't think he would go that far."

"We can only hope."

Finally, she decided to let it go. She cleaned up her mess, came back into the living room and poured herself another glass, which she downed in one shot.

Before she said a word, she pointed at the camera. "Is it recording what we say, as well?"

He shrugged. "I don't think so, but I don't know for sure."

Just to be safe, she leaned over and turned up the volume on the small stereo system. A U2 song that always brought tears to her eyes—Miss Sarajevo—was playing but she tried to tune it out and focus on Nico. In low voices, they continued discussing the possibility of getting to a vehicle and escaping.

"What about the garage down the hill?" Gabriella asked.

One time, not long after her escape attempt, she had headed that direction but Esmeralda had whistled loudly to let her know she was watching.

Fear of the woman reporting back to the man in the mask—and that he might follow through on his earlier threat—sent her back to the house.

"I have walked down there," he said. "All the doors were locked."

"You walked down there? Why didn't you tell me?" Her voice was sharp. "I thought we were in this together, but you apparently aren't including me in anything."

Nico looked away for a minute. He pulled at his shirtsleeves and sighed, turning back. "I can tell you one thing but it won't help us."

He leaned forward conspiratorially. "I heard Esmeralda tell someone the other day that the keys to the vehicles were kept in the garage."

"Really?" She leaned forward.

He held out a hand. "I told you it wouldn't help us. Without the key to the garage, we can't look in the garage for the vehicle keys, can we?"

"All we need to do is get inside the garage, right?"

He looked skeptical. "I suppose. But that's going to be very difficult."

"No, it's that simple," she said and yawned. She didn't explain it would be simple because of her lock picking skills. It was nearly six in the morning. The pink light of sunrise was filtering in through her French doors.

Each night, when dawn broke and they were both nearly falling asleep, Nico would lean over and tenderly kiss her on the cheek before dragging himself to his feet and out the door, leaving Gabriella flushed with lust and guilt, disconcerted by the wave of desire that whisper of a kiss sent coursing through her. It was that damn scar.

Tonight was no different.

"You're falling asleep," he said. "I'll go now."

He leaned over and it seemed as if his kiss was extra warm on her cheek and lingered a little bit longer than normal. She watched him gather up his things through half slit eyes and didn't move until he left, closing her door softly behind him.

Crawling into bed, she was torn by her desire. It was natural to be physically attracted to Nico. Even without the way his eyes devoured her each night, she knew he wanted her, too. But after that first night at the campfire when he kissed her, he had respected her desire to be left alone. Ironically, it made her like him even more because he respected her loyalty to her husband. He didn't mock her belief that as long as there was the most infinitesimal chance that Donovan was still alive, she owed him her fidelity.

She wondered if whoever was watching her through the camera saw her afterward, tossing and turning in the sheets with her lust.

CHAPTER TWENTY-THREE

This morning Monica didn't wake Donovan with her soft kisses. Instead, a man in a white suit and dark sunglasses strutted in and ordered Donovan to stand. Two other men followed, one holding a machine gun he pointed at Donovan, his finger casually resting on the trigger. This man was wiry and fidgety, which made Donovan more nervous than he might have been just seeing the gun. The gunman's finger was trembling, twitchy, on the trigger.

Without a word, one man yanked Donovan's hands behind his back and tied them with something that felt like a bungee cord. He pulled what looked like a feedbag tight over Donovan's head.

This was it. He couldn't recognize the woman in the photo and they were done with him. Donovan swallowed back the metallic taste of fear that filled his mouth. He never knew fear had a taste before. He was disappointed to find that he was petrified to die. He'd always thought he was tougher, braver than this, but right now his knees were in danger of completely giving out, sending him plunging to the concrete floor.

A hand on his back prodded him to walk. He jerked along, worried he would slam into a wall or barrier he couldn't see.

Donovan repressed his urge to struggle. If he tried to get away from the men, in this basement, the man with the gun would shoot him on the spot. It would be messy and not ideal, but that twitching finger on the trigger would not hesitate. Better to wait and try to figure out a way to escape outside somewhere as they led him to his grave.

Donovan tried to take a step and then tripped, falling forward but yanked back by his wrists. He realized they were at the stairs leading out of the basement. Feeling his way with his toe, he managed to scale the stairs.

Hushed voices greeted his caravan as they made their way through the house. Donovan could feel cold stone under his bare feet. Just when he felt the cool morning breeze of an open door or window hit his face, someone kneeled by his feet and pushed his feet into slip on shoes. Briefly, he considered kneeing the person in the face, but the thought that it might be an innocent person, such as a maid, dissuaded him. Not to mention the feel of the automatic weapon's barrel between his shoulder blades.

Why did they care if he had shoes on as they led him to his assassination?

Outside, he stumbled down a few more stairs, with someone gripping his elbows and then he was pushed into the back of a car. He lay there until he felt someone push in beside him. Damn. He started to sit up but was shoved back down into a reclining position.

He strained his ears to listen as they drove. It sounded and felt like the vehicle went from pavement to gravel to dirt. After about fifteen minutes, the car stopped. Donovan was yanked out of his seat and the bag was ripped off his head.

He squinted against the brightness of the sun filtering in through the rainforest canopy above. They were in a small clearing. The man in the white suit led the way, looking back for Donovan to follow.

"*Vamos.*" Let's go.

The man with the gun followed, although he didn't stick the gun against Donovan's back.

The man in the suit led the way through the brush, letting the branches flap back and sting against Donovan's arms. They were hiking up a slight hill and Donovan was soon sweating and winded. He hadn't done more than a few push-ups during his captivity the past few months. Although at first, he had started an exercise regime to stay in shape, depression had soon taken over, leaving him lying on his bed for hours, unable to motivate himself to do anything but drift off.

The only activity he looked forward to each day was Monica's visit where they would spend at least an hour wrapped in one another's arms. Her presence was the only thing keeping him going.

He didn't know who he was. He didn't know how he had got there.

The only clues were snapshots in his dreams that were so hazy he couldn't tell if they were memory or his imagination. They'd told him he was a spy, but he kept getting glimpses of himself in a police officer uniform. And one shocking dream about seeing a group of men gathered around a body in a parking lot, firing bullets into the person.

That was the worst part. For some reason the majority of his memories involved some sort of dead body. It made him wonder if he was an assassin. In one dream, he stood over a beautiful woman on the floor of a cave. Her eyes were wide and unstaring and she had a bullet hole through her forehead.

He would wake from these dreams screaming and sweating.

Now, as the two men led him through the jungle, he knew he would die without figuring out who he was. When the man in front of him pulled up short, Donovan inhaled sharply.

The wreckage site. The body of the plane was somewhat intact. It looked like an eight-seater. There had to be other bodies or victims or survivors somewhere.

Something about the wreckage site made him ill. He leaned

over and vomited, some repressed memory of the crash obviously

didn't sit well with him. The only thing he remembered was coming to

on the ground. When he had regained consciousness, the first thing he

had seen was a man crouched over him peering into his face. He sat up

and looked around, having no idea who he was or where he was or

what had happened. Then he saw the plane. Another man was leaning

over it. A third man was dragging a body down a hill away from them.

The body was bloody and nearly decapitated. Donovan leaned over and

vomited onto the jungle floor.

When Donovan looked up again a man took off running in the

woods, as if he were tracking something or someone.

A gunman kept kicking Donovan asking, "¿Dónde está el?"

Where is he?

"¿Quien?" Who? Donovan kept asking.

The man kicked him in the ribs until Donovan passed out.

Later, when he came around again, the man who had run into the

woods was back, shaking his head.

He said something in Spanish, spitting on the ground, and the

man who had kicked him, leaned down to prop Donovan up against a

tree trunk. He gave him a water jug and then put crude bandages on

Donovan's cuts. Donovan was too sick and exhausted to protest or move. When they helped him stand, he realized his ankle was injured, making it painful to walk. The men helped him down the steep hillside and put him in the back of a car, tugging a bag over his head. He struggled, but felt the butt of a rifle sharp against his temple and then only saw black.

The next time he woke, he was in his basement prison.

This was the first time he'd been outdoors in the months of his captivity. Filling his lungs with fresh air, along with the warmth of the sun and the cool touch of a light breeze on his body made him want to weep. He hadn't realized how much he missed being outside until this exact moment. It was a good thing they were going to kill him because now going back in that basement would be too much, too tough to take. If they hadn't brought him out here to kill him and tried to put him back in that dark, dank basement, he would fight and they would kill him then anyway.

Donovan glanced over at that man with the gun. He leaned lazily on a tree trunk, eyelids half slit. The other man was poking around at the wreckage site, kneeling to dig through a backpack that had obviously already been searched.

Every once in a while, the men shot a glance at Donovan. He didn't know what they expected of him or what they were waiting for. He stared hard at the plane, hoping that some type of memory would flood his consciousness, but the only memory of this spot he had was when the men found him. He walked over to the plane, expecting to be stopped at any second, but the man near the fuselage backed up and gestured for Donovan to go ahead.

Donovan peered inside, searching for anything that looked familiar. Nothing. It was just the inside of a plane. With a few bits of metal streaked with rusty dried blood. Two backpacks were outside the plane, but had been turned upside down and emptied out. He crouched awkwardly nearly tipping over to peer at the contents scattered on the ground. Donovan was sure most of the belongings already had been scavenged.

After a few minutes, he heard some rustling in the brush. Then a face appeared. This man wore a Mardi gras mask and spoke heavily-accented English. Donovan saw that every bit of the man's skin was covered. Even his hands were covered in black silk gloves. Six men with automatic rifles flanked him.

As the masked man stepped into the small clearing, the two men with automatic rifles stood to either side of him.

The masked man stood eerily still until everyone had settled and were watching him expectantly. Then he spoke.

"Good day, Mr. Donovan."

Donovan drew back with a jolt. His name was Donovan. He knew the man was right to call him that, but he shook his head in disbelief. That was his name, but he still didn't have a clue who he was.

"You act surprised," the man said, cracking his knuckles beneath the thin gloves. "Do you recognize your name?"

Donovan nodded, at a loss for words.

"That is your last name."

Donovan raised an eyebrow.

"Your first name is Sean."

The name sent a chord of longing and heartache through him. His name was Sean Donovan. He couldn't help it; he mouthed the name to himself in wonder.

The man saw and chuckled.

"Sean Donovan, this is where we found you. Do you remember anything about this plane or the crash or who you were with?"

Donovan slowly shook his head. He didn't want to tell this man but the moment he heard his name out loud, a sharp memory returned: a woman with red hair, dressed in black, looking down at him and crooning his name—Sean Donovan—in a soothing voice with an Irish accent.

"I'm going to have you remain here for about another hour to see if anything comes back to you. It is very important that you remember these details. Maybe now that you know your name some of your memory will come back."

The man turned and disappeared into the jungle again. His bodyguards waited a few seconds, glaring at Donovan as if he were going to run after the man and attack him. Then they also turned and disappeared into the jungle.

Walking around the crash site, Donovan kicked half-heartedly at the leaves that had fallen from the trees, hoping to unearth some clue. Nothing appeared on the ground, but something did catch his eye near the foot of a small tree.

He shot a glance at the gunman guarding him. The man had his eyes closed behind his sunglasses and was breathing deeply. He was asleep. The man in the white suit had wandered deeper into the jungle. He could hear the rustling brush as the man walked.

For a split-second Donovan thought about taking his chances and running through the jungle, but right when he did, he heard the other man nearby whistling. Maybe he could outrun one gun, but not two.

Instead, he continued casually kicking up dirt and poking around, leaning to look at this and that. Making sure the men weren't watching, Donovan casually leaned down near the tree. He cupped the small rectangular piece of white laminated paper in his and slipped it into the waistband of his pants without glancing at it.

The sun hung low in the sky before they led Donovan through the jungle and back into the basement. Once the door shut on what had become his home, Donovan was filled with relief.

It surprised him. He'd tried to escape from the basement for weeks. And yet when they returned him here, he was happy.

It was because he was still alive.

They hadn't meant to kill him. They were just trying to jog his memory. But it hadn't worked. The only memory that had come to Donovan in the rainforest had been the face of a red-haired woman. Sitting on his futon, he wondered if the woman had been his mother.

As he undressed for bed, the white laminated card fell onto the floor. He quickly stooped to read it. It had his name and picture and read Drug Enforcement Agency. He was a DEA agent, not a cop.

CHAPTER TWENTY-FOUR

Gabriella paused in the doorway of the kitchen.

She spent a while in the bathroom smudging makeup under her eyes to create dark circles. Watching Esmeralda dry a large ceramic bowl, she leaned against the doorjamb and exaggerated a large and loud yawn.

Esmeralda looked up and smiled, setting the bowl down and drying her hands on the dishcloth. *"Pobrecita. Mucho sueno?"*

"Si," Gabriella said. "I cannot sleep though. I have nightmares about my mother and my daughter. Can you please help me? I need to sleep. I am starting to think crazy thoughts."

Esmeralda nodded. *"Si,* no sleep makes crazy people. It is torture in some countries."

"Can you help me?

Esmeralda wrinkled her nose and tilted her head. *"Como?"*

Gabriella mimed putting pills from a cupped palm into her mouth and drinking a glass of water. "Pills. To help me sleep. Please."

Looking off into the distance, Esmeralda frowned. *"Possible. Later."*

Gabriella gave her a grateful smile and went back to her room.

A few hours later, Esmeralda knocked at her door. When Gabriella opened it, Esmeralda looked both ways furtively and then slipped two pills into Gabriella's hand, patting her closed fingers. "Shhh."

"*Gracias*." As soon as Gabriella closed the door, she hurried to the bathroom, shut the door, turned on the taps, and carefully folded the pills in a few squares of tissue paper, tucking it far back in a drawer that contained clean washcloths.

She did that every night for a week until Esmeralda didn't show up one night.

Gabriella stopped in the kitchen on the way to the pool one morning.

Without Gabriella saying a word, Esmeralda shook her head fervently. "*No mas* pills."

"Okay."

#

Earlier, Gabriella had started a load of laundry in the room down the hall, but the clothes were still drying, so when Nico came to her room, instead of wearing her faded tank top and a pair of cotton shorts, Gabriella had searched through the big walk in closet for something else to wear. There was nothing really casual. Most were outfits fancier than she would wear to a formal dinner. Finally, she

decided on a long black dress with tiny straps and a low-cut neck in a

soft cotton material. She slipped that on, kept her feet and face bare and

her hair loose.

When Gabriella opened the door, Nico stepped back and took

her in from her feet to her eyes. She could feel her cheeks flush.

Turning away, she headed for her usual spot on the floor in

front of the fireplace, with her back up against a small sofa. Nico

followed her lead and started to build the fire as he normally did.

But tonight, when he handed her a tumbler of whiskey, his

fingers lingered on hers. She tried to brush it off, but the room was

crackling with their chemistry. It was impossible to ignore. Tonight,

they spoke in low tones, almost languidly about their childhoods.

And then Gabriella asked something that sent Nico leaping to

his feet.

He was talking about learning to swim in the ocean.

"I was such a natural, unlike my son—" he immediately shut

his mouth.

"You're a father?" Gabriella was astonished. She'd spent so

many nights talking about being a mother to Grace. She'd shared

details about how difficult it had been to get pregnant. How horrific it

had been when a madman had kidnapped her daughter. How Grace was her life and how becoming a mother had changed her forever. And yet, he had never once mentioned he was a parent, as well. She's assumed he was childless.

He jumped to his feet and started tearing at his hair, pacing. Not looking at her.

She watched him, confused.

Finally, he stopped pacing and knelt beside her. "I cannot speak of this now."

And like he did every night, he gently kissed her cheek and left. But this time he left hours before the sunrise, leaving Gabriella to toss and turn until dawn, wondering what secrets her new friend was keeping.

Lying in bed, watching the sun rise through the windows to the east, Gabriella found herself face down on her bed, sobbing. Her mother was dying. Donovan was dead. She should just admit it. And for some reason, her captors were keeping her. They had not told her of any demands or hinted that she would ever go home again. Not knowing why they were keeping her prisoner was driving her crazy. And she had to face facts:

This was her life now.

She'd been here at least a month, although it was easy to lose track. Her mother must have told Grace she was dead. Her mother might be dead now, too. Gabriella was never going to see either one of them alive again. The three people she loved most in the world were out of her reach, most likely forever. The realization sent a new wave of despair through her.

She would die without the chance to make it up to Grace. To make amends for her angry outburst. Without a chance to dote on her daughter and listen to every precious word that came out of her daughter's mouth. She would die without being able to say goodbye to her mother, to hold her and thank her for everything.

Her tears were also for her guilt. She'd been a terrible mother to Grace the past few months. After Donovan disappeared, she'd effectively ignored her daughter. The realization hit her like a punch in the gut. Grace had tried to share bits of her day, but Gabriella had tuned it all out, pretending to listen and instead, drowning in her own sea of grief. Now, she could see that Grace saw how unimportant she was during those moments. It was clear that she knew her mother was annoyed by the small interruptions throughout their evening. Grace could probably tell her mother was counting the minutes until she could escape interacting with her daughter and fall into the deep blissful oblivion those sleeping pills brought her in her dark bedroom.

Gabriella cried and begged God for the chance to show Grace her love and to see her mother before she died, if she still was alive.

She prayed for another chance where she would never for one second take her precious daughter's presence for granted, but would instead cherish every moment.

Finally, when her eyes and head hurt from crying, she sat up and washed her face, staring in the ornate antique mirror above the vanity. The resolve in her own eyes, so like her mother's eyes, reminded her of what she needed to accept.

Her mother had given her the words she needed to hear in her letter:

She was a Giovanni. A survivor. She'd faced worse than this before. She had to toughen up, face reality and get on with it. She had to get the hell out of this tropical prison and find her way back to Grace and Maria. And she was going to get Nico to help.

If her life was going to truly be lived without Donovan, then maybe being with Nico was her fate.

CHAPTER TWENTY-FIVE

The brief taste of freedom from being led into the jungle lit a fire under Donovan. He started doing sit-ups, push-ups and pull-ups. His muscles were weak but it felt good to have them burn from his efforts after lying around in the damp basement for weeks.

His name was Sean Donovan.

That knowledge brought some memories sharply into focus, but they seemed to all be from his childhood.

The red-haired woman *had* been his mother. He recognized her. Flashes of her sweet smile came to him often. While he was awake and in his dreams.

But the painful part was he didn't have any recent memories of her. Every memory he had involved looking up at her or clinging to her skirt or her caring for him.

He was disturbed that he had no memories of her when he was an adult.

Had she died when he was young?

Along with the bits and pieces of memories, came increased frustration. It wasn't enough to have tiny flashes that meant nothing.

One night, he woke in a sweat, heart pounding. He'd remembered something from his life as an adult. Well, it was either a memory or a dream.

He was a police officer at a gun range, firing a weapon. He was demonstrating for someone. The next image was him leaning down, arms wrapped around a woman, guiding her hand on the trigger finger. Because of his angle, all he could see was her tousled brown hair next to his. He whispered in her ear. He tried to lean to see her profile, but she turned away.

He could smell her. The scent of her made him wild with lust. But then in the next moment of the dream or memory, he was walking by himself at the range. He caught a glimpse of himself in a nearby window. He stared at his image. Then, suddenly behind him was the woman. He whipped around to see her face. When he did she was gone.

That's when he'd woken up.

The woman from his dream or memory, whichever one it might be, was the woman in the photograph. Her name seemed to slip through a sieve in his mind. Every time he seemed about to grasp who she was, the memory grew vague.

Lying in the dark, other images swarmed his mind.

Flashes of him having a beer with other police. This time none of them were in uniform, but they all—including him—had badges clipped to their belt buckles.

He might be DEA now, but he had been a detective.

But while he was awake there were no more images of the tousled haired woman. It made him wonder if the gun range scene was not a memory, but a dream conjured up from staring at the woman's picture so much, trying to figure out who she was and why his captors wanted him to identify her.

If she was important enough for them to keep him prisoner, she had to be a spy. A top-level spy with critical information that would make or break the drug cartels down here. That is the only reason he was still alive: to identify that woman.

Which made him realize something else—once he did, he'd probably be executed.

CHAPTER TWENTY-SIX

Changing into the black bikini she found in her closet, Gabriella glanced out the window and knew she wouldn't survive an escape attempt on her own. Even if she managed to make it down to the dirt road below, then what? Wait for a passing car and hope they didn't work for the man in the mask?

She wanted to sneak down to the garage and investigate.

Her new plan was to act like she had settled into life as a captive, to pretend to enjoy herself, to pretend to be falling for Nico. Walking around angry and defiant hadn't gotten her any closer to figuring out why she was being held captive.

The wardrobe, the nightly candlelit dinners, the obvious approval of him sneaking into her room every night, all seemed to point to their captor encouraging a romance with Nico. But why?

For now, she'd play along and see what happened. At least that's what she told herself. She was faking an attraction to get him to help her escape. But she knew she was lying to herself. The attraction was real. She could plan her escape without him if she needed.

She slipped out of her room with a tunic covering her bikini and went searching for a beach towel in the small laundry room off the kitchen.

Now, as she crept barefoot along the terra cotta floor, she heard a voice coming from a room that was normally locked. She knew. She had tried every door in the hallway numerous times. The door was cracked a few inches so she peered inside.

Nico was sitting at a large mahogany desk. His chair was swiveled away from her. He was facing a large wall of windows overlooking the jungle below.

He was on the phone.

It was an old-fashioned desk phone with a curly black cord stretching from the handset near his ear to the black phone on the desk.

"Let me talk to him." His voice cracked a little with something. Fear maybe. Then it grew angry. "If you don't put him on the phone right now, it is over. This was our agreement. I've done everything you ask. You do not hold up your end, I do not hold up mine."

In frustration, he swung the chair around to face the desk. Gabriella ducked back just in time. She leaned against the wall near the door, waiting for Nico to call her name or footsteps to head her way.

A clatter at the end of the hallway sent Gabriella toward the small laundry room off the kitchen where she quickly snatched up a large white beach towel and headed for the pool.

She shook with anger.

Nico wasn't acting like a goddamn prisoner. He sat in that office, which was usually locked, and acted like a king. What the fuck was going on?

The betrayal was enormous. She'd trusted him. She'd thought he was on her side, but this was not an even playing field. She wasn't allowed in that room or able to make phone calls, despite her begging the man with the mask to allow her to call her family.

But Nico was allowed.

Everything she'd thought since she arrived here was wrong. But she couldn't let anybody know what she had seen.

Stick to the plan. She headed out to the pool and found a lounge chair that faced the house, so he couldn't miss her. She stripped off the tunic and stretched out, somewhat soothed by the sun soaking into her bones.

Sitting with her sunglasses on to hide her eyes, Gabriella watched Nico come out onto the veranda squinting until his eyes focused on her and a wide smile spread across his face, white teeth brilliant against his dark skin.

She made herself smile back. She would do anything if it increased her chances of escaping. Anything.

But her senses were on high alert. Nico had sat in that office like he belonged there. Not like he was a prisoner like her. He sat there as if it were his own home. And he was talking on the phone. The phone. Gabriella was going to sneak into that office at the next opportunity and try to make a call. She hadn't seen any other phones in the entire hacienda.

And now, as she spread sunscreen along her arms and face and neck, she'd continue with her plan. She'd warm up to Nico, but keep her guard up. When he slid into the lounge chair beside her, tugging off his tight tee-shirt, she couldn't help but sneak a glance sideways at him and realized keeping her guard up was going to be a lot tougher than she'd thought.

One thing she knew for sure was that he desired her. It was clear every time he looked at her, every time they touched, every word he said. On top of that, his glance told her something else. It wasn't just lust. It was more.

That was her advantage, her trump card.

If he had access to the phone, then he was her ticket out of here. She would make it so he wanted to help her. That he would put her in touch with her daughter Grace. That he would help her get home.

She would fuel his desire and use it to her advantage.

When she turned over, Nico offered to spread sunscreen on her back.

"May I? The sun is much hotter here than you are used to. I would hate to see you suffering from sunburn. May I?"

She smiled and nodded. As his hands caressed her back, her body betrayed her. She couldn't help but respond to his touch. That's when Gabriella reminded herself that it was all part of the plan. But deep down in a dark corner of her heart, she knew she'd use her virtuous plan in part to fulfill her own desires.

CHAPTER TWENTY-SEVEN

Monica seemed distracted today. After a rambunctious lovemaking session, she turned away from Donovan on the small futon mattress and buried her face in her hands.

"What is it?" Donovan brushed back her sleek black hair, trying to see her face.

"*El Senor* is bringing another shipment in and I don't think my heart can bear it."

Donovan held his breath. She had never spoken about the "*senor*" or anything besides her own sad past.

At first Donovan thought she must mean a shipment of drugs, but Monica saying she was heartbroken about another shipment of drugs didn't make sense. As soon as he thought this, the horrific answer became clear—another shipment of young women who would be used as drug mules.

He tried to hide his surprise. How did he know this? It was something from his memory. He flashed back to sitting in the seat of an airplane—a large commercial jet, not the small plane he crashed in.

While he sat, he reviewed a stack of photos of gruesome bodies encased in plastic that had been found in an American lake.

Then he remembered, the bodies were young Mexican women who had been transporting some type of drug internally and the method had failed. The containers with drugs they had ingested had burst, killing them instantly. Somebody, maybe the drug lord, had dumped the bodies in the lake.

That must be why he was in Central America. He'd been heading here to stop it from happening again. But he couldn't let Monica realize any of this. Her loyalty to the drug lord was unshakable. He had to play it cool.

"Where are they, Monica? The girls? Is he keeping them here?"

She sat up and angrily brushed her tears away. "Yes. He keeps them here—they have a special princess room on the top floor. They are all so excited. They are giggling and trying on clothes and using makeup and perfume. They think they are so special. They all get to leave here and go to new lives in America, with diamonds and gold and cars."

Donovan didn't correct her.

"Why does this upset you, *mi querido?*"

Without realizing it, he called her his darling. It was what she sometimes called him and it came out automatically. But Monica was still talking and he needed to pay attention if he were going to help those girls.

"He loves them more than me. They are so innocent and sweet and fun and I am just boring old Monica who has to deal with dirty laundry and ..." she closed her mouth abruptly.

"And keeping his prisoner occupied?"

She nodded looking down.

"I need to tell you something," Donovan said, sitting up and raking his hand through his hair. "You should not be jealous of those girls."

Monica looked at him with skepticism.

CHAPTER TWENTY-EIGHT

The red silk dress clung to Gabriella in all the right places. She slipped on the gold sandals and hung dangling earrings from each ear.

Narrowing her eyes as she slicked black eyeliner across her lids, Gabriella thought again about how well the clothes and shoes fit. Proof that somebody knew about her trip to Guatemala. Besides the senator, she couldn't think of anyone else besides her family and friends who knew about her plans.

The color of the dress reminded her of one of her favorite photos of her mother and father. They were dressed to go to a fancy event. Her father wore a tuxedo and her mother wore a low-cut red dress with a diamond necklace. They looked like movie stars. It was before they had kids, years before Gabriella was born.

Thinking of her mother made her sad and angry and determined to get home. She would do whatever it took.

When she closed the door to her room, she caught the faintest sound of giggling. It sounded like a room full of teenage girls having a party. She paused trying to figure out which direction it was coming from, but then the kitchen door swung open and Esmeralda appeared, the blaring sounds of her TV filtering into the hallway. It must have been something on the TV.

Esmeralda made a hurry gesture, pointing Gabriella toward the dining room. Gabriella stepped up the pace. She was a few minutes late tonight. Getting dressed for dinner had taken longer than she had planned.

Walking into the dining room, she felt, rather than saw, Nico freeze when he saw her. It was the first time she had dressed for dinner. His eyes were appreciative, as he stood behind her chair, ready to pull it out.

She folded herself into the chair and Nico pushed it in. His fingers lightly brushed her bare shoulders and his man smell—cologne and something else—swept over her. She swallowed. He was undeniably appealing. But he was dangerous. She must not forget that. This was all part of the plan to get back home to her mother and daughter.

But Gabriella was having a hard time straddling the line between feigning attraction for Nico and true yearning for him to touch her. Every brief touch sent her senses reeling.

Be strong. You are a Giovanni.

Her pep talks to herself grew weaker as dinner went on and the alcohol flowed.

For some reason, maybe in response to her ditching her tank top and cargo pants for the first time, Nico took care to serve her. Each dish Esmeralda brought out, he stood and held the platter for Gabriella to dish up a portion onto her own plate. He stood so close their bodies inevitably brushed against one another, the tiniest touch making hairs of her arms tingle.

Gabriella tried to clear her head, but each course also meant a refill of the wine. This night, rather than one bottle to share, the dinner had started with an aperitif of Campari and soda and then a small glass of prosecco.

"We celebrate your dress," Nico had said before uncorking the prosecco. Now, as they finished their last course of a simple green salad, she could see Nico getting out the Limoncello bottle for dessert.

Her senses were already whirling. The alcohol, oysters, the scallops, the scent of Nico so close, the candlelight, the feel of the silk dress on her thighs. She felt warm, relaxed, and cozy if not a little dizzy.

She heard the sound of laughter and giggling again. It seemed like it was coming from a vent in the wall. Standing, she started to head for the wall to see if she could hear better, but Nico stood and intercepted her, blocking her way. Looking up she met his eyes.

When he leaned forward and rubbed his fingers across her lips, she closed her eyes. When he put his mouth on hers, she didn't object. When he pressed his body to hers, she moaned. He backed her up against a velvet-curtained wall and she let him take his fill of her mouth and then let his lips trail down her body. It was only when he carefully slid the spaghetti straps of her dress off her shoulders that the cold air on her breasts roused her from her lust-filled reverie.

"No." She breathed the word more than spoke it.

He pulled back, searching her face. She knew he saw her sadness and regret, but also her desire. With the lightest touch, he pulled the straps back up on her dress. He nodded his understanding and then leaned down and kissed her forehead before turning and walking away without a word.

His abrupt departure had the opposite affect that she had expected. Instead of feeling relief that the temptation of his body was gone, Gabriella felt an unexpected loss and yearning that made her want to run after him and abandon everything she'd ever known.

#

After dinner, Gabriella waited in her room, still wearing the red dress. At one point, she locked her door with a deadbolt. She couldn't let him in tonight. If he came to her and touched her, she would give in.

Because she didn't know for sure if Donovan was dead, that could

mean she was betraying her marriage vows, being unfaithful.

But she brushed that thought aside. It was time to face that

Donovan was dead. She couldn't be strong any longer. Close to when

Nico usually arrived at ten, she slid the deadbolt open. And stared at the

doorknob. Shortly after ten, she heard footsteps outside her door, but

then they left again. He must have changed his mind, knowing, as she

did, that she was going to give herself to him tonight. He was

protecting her from herself. He respected how she felt unfaithful to

Donovan. This realization made her want him even more.

She slunk on the couch. After another five minutes, she poured

herself some wine out of a bottle in a small mini refrigerator in her

walk-in closet. No matter how much of the wine she drank, there was

always a fresh bottle there the next day.

By ten-thirty, she'd had three glasses when her door opened.

For once, Nico's hair was messed up. He didn't smile when she

rose to greet him.

"I'm sorry I'm late. I didn't want to have to show you this."

He thrust a photo toward her. It was a Polaroid. It revealed only

the bare torso and head of a man lying down sleeping. Gabriella

gasped. It was Donovan.

Donovan's eyes were closed. His face swollen, bruised and beaten.

Gabriella could barely form words. "Where is he?"

Her hands were shaking so much the photograph was wobbling with them. She tried to focus, but her eyes were suddenly blurry.

Nico didn't answer. She looked up and saw it in his eyes before he spoke. She choked back a sob. "I'm so sorry," Nico said. "This is from the morgue. Look at the back."

Staring at the picture in disbelief, Gabriella noticed deep purple circles surrounding Donovan's closed eyes. She had thought they were from a beating. He lay on a darkish slab. He was dead—not sleeping.

She flipped it and written in blue ink it said, "Flores Morgue. Unidentified male."

Gabriella sobbed and tried to punch Nico in the chest with both fists, pounding lightly on his silk shirt before he grabbed both of her wrists. "You bastard. You knew and you didn't tell me? You let me go on thinking he might be alive?"

"I only got this picture today. I was able to break into an office. I found a screwdriver and undid the door handle. This picture was sitting on the desk. I called the Italian embassy for help. They didn't believe who I was. They said the deal was that I didn't even exist, so if I was calling it had to be someone impersonating me. I was going to call the American embassy, but then someone came. I had to

hang up and leave. I was so close, Gabriella. So close to getting us out

of here."

"Then let's go back to the office. Now." Gabriella headed for

the door.

Nico put his hand on her arm.

"That's where I just was. They changed the lock. It's a

deadbolt now. It cannot be opened. Also, they found the screwdriver I

had hidden in my room in a drawer." He drew away, pacing. He

seemed agitated.

Gabriella stared at him through her tears. Maybe he wasn't the

enemy. He admitted to being in the office and said he was there trying

to help them escape.

She was still clutching the photograph in her hand, which was

shaking. When she looked down and saw Donovan's lifeless face, she

closed her eyes.

"I'm so, so sorry," Nico said. "That is why I was late. I was

trying to figure out how to tell you. The last thing I want to do is hurt

you. Don't you understand I would do anything for you, anything to

prevent you from hurting ever again."

He held her and she wept into his shirt, not pulling back until the fabric was soaked. When he started to kiss her tears, tracing the path as they fell down her neck and onto her chest, she clung to him.

When he peeled the dress off her shoulders, she arched her back in pleasure. Donovan was dead. She had her proof now. Nico hadn't lied to her. She'd been strong long enough.

CHAPTER TWENTY-NINE

Slowly, bits and pieces of his previous life returned to Donovan.

Flashes of memory. Knowledge of the jungle regions around him.

Most of the tiny fragments of memory involved him on the commercial airline. He gained glimpses of himself studying a thick briefing folder that contained secret, confiscated maps. He didn't know how he knew the maps were secret and confiscated, but they were.

The maps were all of areas in the Peten jungle. They showed hundreds of "narco-ranches" with dirt runways hidden deep in the jungle where drug lords and their minions ran elaborate smuggling operations. One map also pinpointed an airplane cemetery full of charred small planes that had been used to transport cocaine from other Central American regions.

Donovan tried to grab ahold of these small glimpses and snatches of memory before they drifted away. So far, he knew he was a DEA agent working on some operation in the Peten jungle of

Guatemala. And he used to be a cop. His mother had red hair. Other than that, he wasn't sure about much else.

Each morning, he tried to subtly draw information out of Monica.

"I know we are somewhere in the Peten jungle," he'd say. "I'm just curious—are we closer to Mexico or El Salvador?"

Monica would look down and swallow. "I'm not supposed to talk about that."

"It can't possibly hurt, could it?" He argued. "It's not like I'm going anywhere. I'm stuck in this basement. A prisoner. I've seen daylight once in God knows how many months or days."

He tried to hide his frustration and anger. After all, it wasn't Monica's fault, but the fury inside was building. His depression was slowly turning into rage. He needed to know more. Much more.

These brief glimpses of memory were only the beginning. He needed to remember more to figure out who was holding him captive, why, and where he was—information he was sure would help aid his escape. If he knew what they wanted, he could use that against them to escape.

It was clear his captors wanted one thing of him—to remember. To remember who the woman in the photo was and to remember who he was. But why?

One day blended into another.

Each day no different than the last.

Today, he woke and waited for Monica to bring him breakfast.

He needed to figure out a way to outsmart the people keeping him prisoner. To do that, he needed to remember who he was. His brain was becoming clearer every day. Not only in terms of his memory, but his thinking in general.

Right after the plane crash, when he first was taken prisoner, his thinking, his brain, was fuzzy. He couldn't hold onto thoughts for very long. And he slept. Long hours. He would wake each morning, stay up for a few hours and then fall into a deep sleep that often lasted until it was dark again. Then, he'd stay up for a few more hours to eat and then fall back asleep.

It must have been part of his recovery from the trauma of the crash. He'd obviously suffered quite a brain injury if he couldn't even remember his own goddamned name. He was filled with such fury and yet, wasn't even sure where to direct his anger.

Sometimes he'd bunch up the flimsy pillow onto the middle of his thin futon and punch it over and over.

CHAPTER THIRTY

Clutching the photo with knuckles turning white, Donovan closed his eyes taking a second to compose himself. Don't let on. Even though it felt like a blade had entered his chest, he had to hide that he recognized the woman in the photo. He recognized his wife, Gabriella.

It was the third picture of his wife they'd shown him during his captivity, every once in a while bringing a new one in for his perusal. His wife.

"Donovan." Monica placed her hands on his shoulders, kissing his neck. "Do you recognize her yet? The beautiful lady?" She purred in his ear, her breath hot on his neck.

Instinctively, he knew he had to pretend he hadn't recognized Gabriella.

"No." he forced himself not to fling her off him. Her nails clinging to his arms, her body pressed tight against his back, all of it was now repulsive. He had to pretend everything was the same. That he didn't know who he was. That he didn't know Gabriella. He couldn't let on.

That's why he turned and took Monica in his arms pressing his mouth to hers. Nothing could change until he figured out what was going on. He had to play along. But his body wouldn't respond. Even with Monica sprawled naked before him licking him in ways that had propelled him into a near out-of-body ecstasy just yesterday.

But today—nothing. All he could think about was Gabriella. Where was she in that photo? Where was he? Only tiny fragments of memory were accessible to him—something about a plane taking off from San Francisco Airport and very little after that.

He needed to clear his head. Stay smart. Stay alive.

Right now, that meant making love to this woman the same way he did every day. Thinking that, realizing that he'd betrayed his wife over and over, sent a stabbing pain through his heart. He had to forget about that for now.

It didn't take long for Monica to notice his lack of enthusiasm.

"*Mi amore*," she pulled back, searching his eyes. "Are you okay?"

"I stayed up too late last night," he said. "I'm a little bit tired."

Was that a flicker of suspicion in her eyes?

He leaned down and kissed her. "I'm sorry. The caffeine in the *café con leche* you brought me is kicking in now though and I'm starting to feel more awake already. Let's try again."

This time when he leaned down and put his mouth on Monica, he closed his eyes and imagined Gabriella in his arms. He could almost smell his wife. His desire grew so strong he picked up Monica and carried her around the small basement bedroom, pressing her against the floor, walls, the bed, and the seat of the chair.

When they were done, she leaned back, panting with a satisfied smile. "You should stay up late more often, my love."

#

After Monica left, Donovan made a fist to punch his pillow in frustration and guilt and fear, but instead at the last second thrust it up into the air and strutted around the basement as if he were doing a victory march. He didn't know where or how, but he knew he was being watched. Every action was monitored. He had to act 24/7, or they would know he recognized Gabriella.

To reinforce his supposed satisfaction with the virulent lovemaking session he'd just experienced, he plastered a self-satisfied, smug smile on his face.

Inside, however, he felt like he was going to vomit. The guilt was suffocating. And it was two-fold. He felt crushing guilt that he was having sex with someone other than his wife, but then he felt ashamed that he was using Monica to keep up the ruse. It was shitty no matter how you looked at it.

As soon as it grew dark, when any hidden cameras would have difficulty seeing what he was doing, Donovan gathered up the other photos, which had become the most precious objects in his world. Holding them up to the thin trail of light coming in the basement window, he searched the photos for clues as to where they were taken.

One picture was of Gabriella in a tank top and cargo pants with a baseball cap pulled low over her eyes. She was speaking to a man with dark hair but the man's back was to the camera. The man wore black pants and a white dress shirt and his hair curled at his neck. It looked like they were outside near a stand of trees. Possibly a jungle.

Another photo showed her in a red dress that fell to her ankles. She was leaning against a wall, holding a tumbler and smiling at someone just out of the frame.

In this one, Gabriella was in a black bikini and big straw hat lying by a pool. A dark-haired man was rubbing sunscreen onto her back. Donovan could only see the man's profile. There was a long scar running down the man's cheek.

Gabriella's skin was the darkest he'd ever seen. Behind her was a large house with giant white pillars and off to one side, he could see a palm tree. Where was she? He squinted and could see jungle behind them.

An overwhelming sensation of danger and fear trickled through him.

They were going to hurt her. There was a reason they'd been asking if he recognized her for the past few months. That is why he had to hide his recognition, no matter what it took.

He spent the rest of the night awake in his futon plotting his escape. He had to find Gabriella. The door at the top of the basement was reinforced and dead bolted from the outside. It would be impossible to break it down by brute force. His only hope was to somehow get the door to the basement opened and then overpower the men waiting behind it. He didn't know how many men there were. He didn't know if they were armed. He was outnumbered and weaponless. He'd have to outsmart them. That was his only chance.

The next morning when Monica handed him a new photo, he barely hid his shock.

There was no doubt. It was a picture of his wife making love to another man, the man with the scar.

To hide his horror, he smirked and grabbed Monica in a kiss, burying his face in her sweet-smelling hair, flinging the picture aside and telling her the picture had turned him on.

He wondered if his captors suspected he had recognized Gabriella and had given him this picture to provoke a reaction.

Concentrating on sex with Monica, pretending she was his wife, Gabriella, was his only strategy to avoid the anguish he was sure would show on his face and through his body language.

Later, when they were done, he leaned back against the pillow propped on the wall and watched Monica sleep. Every day when she came inside the room, she knocked on the door after she closed it, said something in Spanish and Donovan could hear the sound of a sliding deadbolt on the other side. When she left the basement, she knocked on the door at the top of the stairs, said something else in Spanish and the door was opened. Donovan never saw what was on the other side during the brief moments the door opened enough for her to slip out. The door was never opened wide enough for Donovan to see what was on the other side.

If he were a more ruthless man, he could fashion some type of weapon and hold it to her neck. He could take her to the top of the stairs and tell her to make the guard open up or he would kill her. To make it believable, he knew he had to really be willing to do just that.

But he didn't have it in him. Maybe he could've before she told him the story of her rape and rescue.

At least that's what he told himself—that his pity for her stopped him from using her as a hostage. But the truth was he had started to fall for her. It was the last thing he wanted to admit. He not only was betraying Gabriella physically, but also emotionally, in his heart.

Monica stretched and opened her eyes and he absentmindedly leaned down to kiss her forehead. Yes, it was much more than lust. She curled herself up in a ball against his side and he wrapped an arm around her protectively. She was sweet and sexy and fun.

He leaned down. "Do you ever leave here?" He gestured above them. "Ever leave this place, this house? Ever meet other people your age?"

She shook her head. She seemed surprised. "Why?"

"To find a husband? To make friends? Do you ever get lonely?"

Monica thought about it for a moment. "I used to," she looked down as she said it. "Before you came."

It made his heart heavy to hear those words. He had no plans to stick around. But right at that moment, he would do anything to Monica happy. Maybe she could escape with him? But he knew that was impossible. Gabriella was his wife. His soul mate. The mother of his child. He would never leave her. He didn't want to leave her. But he couldn't have it all. He knew that when, not if, but when, he escaped, he would leave a little piece of his heart behind with Monica.

Despair filled him. It wasn't fair. It wasn't right. How could he feel this way about two different women? Any anger he had toward Monica about her role in his captivity had evaporated. She was an innocent pawn. She was, in fact in many ways, as much a captive as he was.

CHAPTER THIRTY-ONE

The sound of helicopters woke Gabriella. Their bone-rattling thud appearing in her dreams as warriors pounding warning signals on drums.

Nico was gone from her bed. The memory of kissing his scar and his lips and his body made her flush. But the sound outside was growing closer.

Once she figured out that the helicopters were coming closer, another sound startled her. It was a loud metal clanking noise right outside her French doors. Jumping up, she yanked open the floor to ceiling curtains only to see her windows had been blocked by steel plates. She raced to the other window, overlooking the jungle below. A steel plate had also fallen into place over the glass.

Next, she placed her ear to her door, listening for sounds in the house. Shouting and then a volley of what sounded like automatic gunfire made her draw back slightly, but then when it didn't get closer, she crouched and put her ear to the door.

Somewhere outside, there was more gunfire and screams and yells, doors slamming, men shouting. More than anything she wanted to go find Nico. It was more than she didn't want to be alone right now. It wasn't that she wanted his protection. If anything, she was worried about his safety. She had no idea who was attacking the hacienda, but by the sounds outside, people were dying and doing so in painful ways. She wondered if when it was over, she'd be next. Her eyes searched her room for a weapon, but she knew there was nothing. She'd already done this when she first arrived.

Crouched with her ear growing numb pressed to the door, she listened and tried to make sense of the chaos outside her door. Footsteps and voices came closer.

What she heard sent a cold chill down her body. It was Nico's voice. Giving orders. Just like she suspected, he'd lied to her. He wasn't a prisoner. He was responsible for her being here. She had made love to him and this was her punishment. He was a liar and a thief and he had betrayed her in the worst way possible.

After several minutes listening to Nico shouting orders, directing people to the helipad, to the garage and ordering them to get more guns, Gabriella felt sick.

She had been such a fool.

Then she heard it. This time for sure: the sound of women screaming and crying. She hadn't imagined the voices. There were other people here that were kept hidden away somewhere. She strained to hear where the noises were coming from, but couldn't tell. The hacienda was large. She'd thought that maybe the drug lord's private quarters took up the entire second floor, so that could be where the other women were, as well.

The sound of voices was lost as the gunfire drowned everything else out.

The gunfight went on for another thirty minutes and then stopped so abruptly it was eerily silent. The sound of a helicopter made the lamps in her room vibrate and then the noise grew fainter as it flew away.

Gabriella leaped to her feet as soon as she heard the sound of footsteps coming down the hall toward her room.

CHAPTER THIRTY-TWO

Donovan crouched up against the door leading out of the basement, his head pressed to the crack under the door, trying to hear what was going on in the rest of the house. He'd been awoken by the nearly deafening sounds of automatic gunfire, hovering helicopters and shouting.

At first, he'd pulled himself up to one of the tiny block glass windows near the basement ceiling. He saw figures moving on the other side. It seemed like there were some greenish colors, but that didn't necessarily mean U.S. military. It could have been a rebel uniform, as well.

After a while, when movement had stopped outside his window, and the noises seemed to move inside, above his head, he scaled the stairs of the basement and tried to hear what was going on. It was as if there was a war right outside his basement prison. People had died. He could hear voices and screams. It sounded like a room full of screaming teenage girls. He also heard voices that sounded English, vaguely military in nature, if it was possible to identify that pattern of speech. He couldn't make out the words, but he swore he heard his

name. Sean Donovan.

Although he didn't have any way to prove it, but he suspected

it was somebody sent from the U.S. government or military trying to

rescue him?

When some of the voices came close, he began kicking at the

door and shouting. "In here. Help me. I'm a prisoner. Help. This is

Sean Donovan. Help." He shouted until his voice grew hoarse, the

footsteps had moved away, and it had grown silent on the other side of

the door.

The fighting had only lasted about thirty minutes. After, the

only noise was the creaking of footsteps on the floor above, which was

a normal sound. He had figured out by the sound of running water that

he was below a kitchen. A large one, it appeared. He'd hear the tapping

of heels and the creaking of the floorboards above him around

breakfast, lunch, and dinner times.

Now, he heard water running and the murmurs of voices above.

He heard the sound of a helicopter and could tell it was leaving

instead of coming.

Whatever had happened outside had sent his adrenaline racing,

but now it was over. It was back to the tedium of his basement prison.

He collapsed on his futon.

The possibility that someone from his government had been trying to rescue him, gave him hope. If they knew he was here, they'd send more troops.

The DEA knew that there were dozens of secret ranches owned by drug runners and lords hidden throughout the Peten jungle. Finding them was another matter. Many, if not all, had massive camouflage nets over the buildings to disguise them from aircraft or satellite. He'd also heard murmuring of some futuristic technology that created a false image of jungle canopy across the compound. Trees surrounding a top-secret area could shoot holograms that created an image only seen from above. He hadn't been able to scope out his prison, to see if this was true for this house.

Then again, there was also a very good chance that the gunfight had been between different factions of drug cartels. That was nothing new. The war was constant.

But he swore he heard English being spoken. And maybe it was his imagination, but it had sounded like someone had said his name.

His countrymen. A surge of hope raced through him.

It was just a matter of time.

He rolled off his futon and did push-ups until he couldn't catch his breath anymore. He needed to be prepared for a fight. While his muscles were still slightly defined, over the past few months he'd

grown soft and complacent from his depression.

Lying exhausted after his makeshift workout, Donovan stared

idly at the block glass basement window. Then sat up. Several fat furry

legs squeezed through a tiny crack around the glass block window.

Holy shit was that one big motherfucking spider. He immediately

recognized it as a Wandering Spider, also known as a Banana Spider—

the deadliest spider in these parts, maybe the world.

Relieved he had spotted it during the day and not at night,

Donovan made a plan. He grabbed the metal bucket from the floor.

He knocked the spider down by whipping his shirt up against

the wall. It took a couple of swipes but the spider fell to the earth

below. After it hit the dirt, it reared up its hind legs and scuttled toward

Donovan, who stood his ground, poised, waiting and watching. When

the spider was about a foot away from his bare leg, Donovan dropped

the bucket on it. He scooted the bucket up against the wall so he

wouldn't trip on it in the night. For the first time since he'd been

captured, Donovan felt a tiny sliver of hope, a tiny nugget of power. He

had a weapon. A mostly uncontrollable, unreliable weapon, but a

weapon nonetheless.

CHAPTER THIRTY-THREE

Gabriella stood facing her door, listening to the footsteps grow closer, waiting to see who was on the other side. With a clattering of keys, her door was unlocked and Nico stood before her, hair messed up and shirt soaked in blood.

She hoped her fury and mistrust didn't show in her eyes. She couldn't let on she knew anything.

But he was in no condition to notice her mood.

He collapsed into the room.

"Oh my God, are you okay?" Despite her anger, Gabriella found she was truly worried. She led him to the bed, where he sprawled out. He winced as she pulled the fabric of his shirt away from a large patch of blood. Beneath his clothes, was a small bullet hole.

"Lean forward."

Supporting him, she glanced at his back near his shoulder where there was a small exit wound. The bleeding was minimal. It only needed a small dressing. This would work out perfectly.

"You're lucky. In and out. Stay right here." She raced to the hallway and glanced down it both ways. Nobody was in sight. Quickly, she closed and locked her door.

"I'll be right back. I think I saw a first-aid kit in the bathroom."

His eyes were closed but he nodded. On the way into the bathroom, she

swooped up a partially full whiskey bottle and hid it in front of her

body as she walked.

Inside the bathroom, she closed the door just enough where

Nico couldn't see what she was doing. Reaching into the back of a

drawer, she retrieved the small folded tissue with the sleeping pills.

Some measure of propriety kept the homeowner from watching

her in the bathroom. He'd made a mistake.

Placing the pills in the bottom of a water glass, she crushed

them with the end of her toothbrush. She poured three fingers of

bourbon into the glass, grabbed the first aid kit from a drawer and

headed back to the bed.

"You doing okay?" As she leaned over, he wrapped his arm

around behind her, caressing her back and gave her a wry smile.

"Much better now."

"Knock it off. You're hurt." She forced a smile.

"It's not so bad," he said, but she could see the effort had cost

him and he grunted with pain as he moved his arm back down.

"What the hell happened out there?" she asked, gently his shirt

even further away from his wound.

"Apparently, our host has enemies who thought he might be here—I think maybe the Gulf Cartel members? I'm not sure. They attacked by dropping assassins into the compound by helicopter. Luckily, our masked friend had been warned of the attack and without us knowing, had armed henchmen waiting. It was a bloodbath."

Gabriella stopped what she was doing and stared. "How did you happen to get involved?"

He swallowed.

"I made the foolish mistake of stepping out of my room to see what was going on. I hadn't even stepped a foot when a gunman turned down the hall and fired. I was able to duck back into my room and lock the door. I stayed there, bleeding on myself until the gunfire had stopped. I am afraid to look around anymore. I first went to the kitchen to look for Esmeralda to make sure she was okay. I couldn't find her, but one of our host's men told me she was safe, so I rushed to find you. I stepped across three bodies on my way here."

Gabriella didn't believe a word he said, but played along. She uncapped the bottle of whiskey.

"What's going on out there now? Maybe we should go investigate? By the way this might sting a little."

Nico cringed as Gabriella dumped some of the whiskey on his wound.

"Oh, *mama mia!*" he cried and tried to sit up.

"Sorry, need to make sure the wound is clean before I put the bandage on. I got the steps out of order. Drink first."

She helped prop him up in the bed, his back resting on pillows and handed him the water glass full of whiskey.

He downed all but a half-inch. She set the glass on the nightstand wondering if all the sleeping pill powder was at the bottom in the remaining liquid.

She was gentle as she dried the skin around the wound and placed the bandage on.

"You rest, I'm going to go see what's going on." She pushed him down on the bed when he tried to sit up. Maybe he didn't drink any of the powder. She eyed the glass again. It did look like some white residue remained.

His eyelids were growing droopy though, as if it was hard to keep them open.

"Nico?" she said softly, waiting for him to meet her eyes.

"Yes?" He gave her a sexy smile.

"I thought I heard voices. Like young women or girls. Do you know what that is about? Are there other girls being held prisoner like us? Are there girls who are staying here as guests of *El Senor*? I swear I've been hearing voices?"

She waited. Here was his chance to tell her.

He raised a hand and made a disparaging noise, sweeping her questions away. "Nah. Nobody. Just us."

He was lying. His voice was becoming slurred as if he was drunk. The pills must be kicking in.

Gabriella pressed on. "You wouldn't lie to me, would you, Nico." She used his name on purpose, calling him out, hoping he would tell her the truth.

"Tell me about your scar. How did you get it?"

"Ah, it was something silly, stupid, really. I was mugged when I was a teen."

Gabriella felt strangely deflated. She'd built it up into something daring, imagined something dangerous, some covert secret operation where he refused to talk and was sliced for it. Instead, he was simply a victim, like anybody else could end up.

"You wouldn't lie to me, would you?" She tried again.

"I was married before," he said, his words slurring together.

"Yes, you told me." Gabriella tried to hide her frustration. "The girls—they are holding other people here aren't they?"

"No," he tried to sit up again and his voice was angry. "Before. To the love of my life."

Gabriella paused. Was he saying he lied about having married for money before? Why was he telling her this? She needed to figure a way to get him to drink the rest of the whiskey without tasting the powder.

His eyes were closed and it seemed like he was growing sleepy, but he kept talking. "Francesca. We were high school sweethearts. We married when we were just kids, just graduated. I loved her so much. We lived near the sea. It was such a simple life. We were poor and we did not care. We had next to nothing, but it was the richest I've ever been in my life."

Gabriella couldn't help it; she perched on the edge of the bed to hear the rest. But before she did, she poured another slug of whiskey in the glass.

"Tell me about her."

"She was stunningly beautiful. She had these big black eyes and black curly hair and the pinkest lips. But she was more beautiful inside. She worked as a midwife in our village. She loved babies so much. It was very hard for her to get pregnant."

Gabriella's stomach clenched a little.

"Every single day of my life I want to die without her." He began to cry. Tears dripped down the sides of his face onto the pillow.

"Today, when I got shot I was happy. I thought, 'Today is the day I get to see my love.'"

Reaching over, Gabriella took Nico's hand in hers and stroked his palm.

His eyes flew up, startling her. "But then I didn't want to die. Do you know why?"

She shook her head wordlessly.

"Because of you," he said, grabbing her hand and kissing it wildly. "I did not know I could love a woman again."

Lifting his head, she made him drain the glass, cringing a little when she saw some white powder at the bottom—the remnant of the sleeping pills.

She put the glass on the far side of the nightstand where he couldn't see it and pulled a blanket up to his chin.

"You should rest," she said.

"God, I miss her so much," his words came out as a sob.

Despite herself, even though she knew not to get involved or care or feel bad, she couldn't help but ask Nico the question. "What happened to Francesca?"

"She died. In childbirth."

"You have a child." Maybe he would tell her now. She waited for him to answer. Instead, his mouth dropped open and a snore emerged. He was asleep.

Time to go find that phone.

Cautiously she opened her bedroom door. The hallway was silent. As she made her way down toward the room that housed the office and phone, she noted that there was not a spot of blood in front of Nico's room where he had claimed to be shot. She tried the door handle. It was locked.

At the office door, she made the sign of the cross, and tried that door. It was also locked. If only she had her lock-picking kit. She'd search the kitchen for something that could be used instead. She needed a tension wrench and a pick.

But right when she was about to walk away, she felt someone nearby. She whirled. At the end of the hallway was a man with an AK-47. Gabriella had fired one at range once and had gone home with a shredded target and sore trigger finger.

He said something in Spanish.

"*No Comprendo*," she said.

Shouting something in Spanish over his shoulder, the gunman kept his eyes on Gabriella. Soon Esmeralda appeared. "He says you go back to your room now. It is still dangerous. We will eat at *siete*."

Gabriella paused. What would the man do if she disobeyed? What if she ran outside? She shot a sideways glance at the door off to her left. It led outside to the veranda. The man with the gun saw and took a threatening step forward.

"Please, miss. Please do as he says." Esmeralda wrung her hands. That was enough for Gabriella to realize the man with the gun was serious. She debated asking Esmeralda about the girl's voices she had heard. Instead, she returned to her room and locked the door. She curled up on the bed beside Nico, her back to him and tried to nap.

#

Nico woke at three complaining of a splitting headache. Gabriella set down the book she'd been reading and tried to act innocent.

"You must've needed that sleep." She smiled and hoped he didn't realize it was an act. Every ounce of attraction she'd ever felt for him had disappeared. It'd been replaced with suspicion and anger that he was lying to her. At the very least, he was complicit in keeping her prisoner here by not telling her the truth. At the worst, he was in on it from the start. The question was why.

Nico groaned as he pulled himself up from the bed.

"I need to go shower, change. I will see you at dinner."

He seemed grumpy. It made Gabriella worry that he knew he'd been drugged.

Did he remember how she pressed him about the girl's voices? He left her room without another word. She waited with her ear pressed to her door until she heard the jingle of keys and heard his door open and close. He had keys to his room and the office, apparently. He was not to be trusted. Not one bit.

As soon as she heard his door shut, she opened hers, closing it silently behind her and raced to the door at the end of the hall. The one that would lead outside closest to the garage. Peering out before she opened the door, she made sure the gunmen weren't still waiting. About an hour before she'd heard the sound of several vehicles and many raised voices and then the noises had all faded. She hoped that meant everyone had left.

Outside on the veranda, she saw a couple wet, stained spots where bodies or blood might have lain. She shuddered as she walked past them, making a wide circle around them. She had been in such a hurry to get to the garage, she hadn't worn shoes and only had on the shorts and tank top she'd slept in.

Now, she crept down some steps and ran toward the garage, looking around as she did. Nobody was in sight. Once she got to the level where the garage was, nobody could see her unless they were also on that level of the driveway so she relaxed a little and slowed down. She kept an eye on the twelve-foot high stone wall, imagining a jaguar scaling it and watching her even though she knew it was unlikely. That's why the wall was there after all.

Circling the garage, she first tried the one door. It was locked.

Damn. Again, she wished for her lock pick kit.

She'd have to forage some materials out of the kitchen and try to come up with her own tools to pick locks. That was the only solution. If only she knew how to hot wire a car, she wouldn't have to worry about step two of her plan—finding keys to the vehicles inside the garage. Why she'd never asked Donovan to teach her this skill, she didn't know. It was ironic that although he knew how to hotwire a car, he'd always frowned on her lock picking skills.

Thinking of Donovan sent a sob into her throat. She wanted to collapse right there on the gravel driveway, but knew she had to keep fighting to get back home to Grace.

After staring at the door in frustration for a few minutes, she headed back to the house.

The kitchen was empty. Quickly, she pulled drawers and flung open cupboards. If someone walked in, she'd plead hunger. She was looking for something like a meat thermometer with a long pointy end.

Or even a bamboo skewer would work. Nothing. There was one drawer that had a lock on it. Maybe the knives were kept in there.

A small drawer had a small stack of papers. Manuals for the refrigerator, oven and microwave. Somebody was very organized. She was about to throw the stack of papers back in when she saw the glint of metal. A paperclip. She could use it as a tension wrench. She only needed one more tool and her lock picking kit would be complete.

Hearing footsteps, she grabbed a glass and turned on the sink faucet. When Esmeralda walked in she was downing the last sip of water. She smiled over the glass.

Esmeralda looked around the kitchen as if suspecting something but then seeing nothing amiss, smiled back. Gabriella noticed something. The woman wore bobby pins to keep her bun in place.

Gabriella lifted her hair off her neck and sighed. "It is so hot."

Then, as if she had just thought of it turned to Esmeralda.

"Do you have a bobby pin?"

Esmeralda looked at her confused. Gabriella pointed to the two bobby pins holding back the woman's hair. Esmeralda nodded understanding.

"*Uno minutos.*"

A few minutes later, Esmeralda returned with a smile and
gently pushed Gabriella's hair back from her face with two bobby pins.
As soon as the door closed again, Gabriella yanked them out of her
hair. Unlike Esmeralda's plain ones, these were coated in pink plastic.
But they would do.

#

That night, Nico didn't come to her room. It was the first time
since they had been kidnapped. Gabriella waited, checking the clock
every few minutes. Finally, when it was nearly midnight, she threw a
sweater on over her tank top and slipped on some ballet flats. The
garage was out. But the office with the phone still beckoned. She would
keep trying it, hoping one time it would be open.

But when she tried to open her door, it was locked.

She was stunned. Someone must have known about her foray
to the garage today. Nico seemed like the most likely suspect. She
thought back to his odd behavior earlier in the dining room. That would
explain it. He knew she had tried to get into the garage.

At dinner that night, she noticed that when she wasn't looking
directly at him, he was studying her. As if he was a little bit suspicious
of her. Once she caught him in the mirror watching her with narrowed
eyes. When she met his gaze, he quickly winked or smiled.

Gabriella went to the three long windows in her room that opened up to a spot on the veranda. Locked. What the fuck? She was a prisoner in her room. She could break the glass. For a second, she eyed a huge black onyx Buddha statue on the floor by the window. She leaned over. It would be tough, but she could lift it high enough to toss it at the window. She set it back down. That wouldn't do. She didn't want everyone to know she was trying to escape. It needed to be sneaky. They couldn't know she was gone until she'd had a chance to reach the main road.

Crawling into bed, she made a plan. Somehow, she would get to that phone and she would call someone.

CHAPTER THIRTY-FOUR

It was later, some indeterminate time deep in the night when Donovan was awakened by heavy footsteps coming down the stairs. He sat up in the dark. He couldn't make out any faces, only caught glimpses of heavy combat boots and pants torn at the ankle revealed in the beam of the flashlight.

A lamp was lit and Donovan saw it was three men, all without masks. He wondered if this time they would kill him. But instead of speaking, the three men holding guns stood back along the walls, as if assigned posts to watch him. He sat up, running his hand through his hair to get it out of his face. When he heard the door to the basement open again, he moved closer to his overturned bucket with the spider underneath and stood, waiting.

First shiny black shoes appeared on the stairs. Then, pressed black slacks and a blazer and ruby-encrusted gold cufflinks came into view. Then, a crisp white shirt and blood red tie. Above that was a face that made his blood boil.

It was the man who was making love to his wife in that picture. The man with the scar. Donovan's fists clenched and it took all his willpower not to attack the man. In an instant, he forgot about his plan

not to reveal he recognized Gabriella. He only remembered when he

saw the man note his clenched jaw and steely gaze.

"Aha," the man said in a thick accent. "You do remember now,

don't you?"

Donovan glared.

"She's quite something, isn't she?" the man said.

If he could, if there hadn't been three men with guns, Donovan

would've killed the man on the spot. With his bare hands.

"I would like to tell you if you cooperated, she'd be yours

again, but I can't say that," the man continued, his eyes never leaving

Donovan. "Because at this point, whether she is yours or not is up to

her. Not me. She might have changed her mind in the past few weeks.

Women can be fickle."

Without seeming to, Donovan took in the posture of the three

gunmen. They were lazy, slouched, not really anticipating any action.

After all, what kind of idiot would try to escape three gunmen in a

small room? But Donovan was making a plan. If he could make it to

one of the gunmen without being shot, he could grab the gun and

without even taking it away from the man, use it to shoot the other two.

It could be done. The wild card was the dude with the Italian accent. He

might be armed or able to intervene.

He needed a distraction. A noise from above provided that for a second. All four men looked up at the stairs. It sounded like a scream. While they looked away, Donovan took his foot and lifted up the bucket a few inches, praying that the spider would head the opposite way instead of attacking his bare foot. To his relief, the spider seemed disoriented and stumbled in the opposite direction toward one of the gunmen. Donovan tried not to look at the spider, but watched out of the corner of his eye as it made a steady path toward the gunman's leg. Donovan watched in disappointment as the spider scaled the wall behind the man.

The gunman closest to Donovan wasn't really paying attention. He had spotted the picture of Gabriella on the floor where Donovan had tossed it in a move he hoped had seemed nonchalant. It was the picture of his wife making love to the fucker standing on the stairs right now. The gunman kept glancing down at it and then back at the man on the stairs, putting the pieces together. The gunman was apparently as surprised as Donovan that his boss was fucking Donovan's wife.

Then, Donovan got a lucky break. The gunman closest to the stairs leaned back against the wall. A second later, he howled, clutching the back of his neck.

The spider.

CHAPTER THIRTY-FIVE

The first aid kit in Gabriella's room was somewhat old-fashioned. It contained syrup of Ipecac. When Grace was a baby, all the books had said to keep this around in case a child ingested poison. It would make you vomit. Doctors didn't recommend this anymore since overdosing on it was so easy. But Gabriella wasn't worried about that.

Now, with the bathroom door locked, Gabriella got ready.

It took a while for her to straighten the bobby pin. The plastic coating was a problem for lock picking. After about twenty minutes she'd stripped the plastic off the bobby pin with her teeth, leaving little shards of pink everywhere that she wiped up and flushed down the toilet.

When she was done, she messed up her hair, tangling it in knots and applied black makeup to create faint shadows under her eyes.

Then she crawled back in bed and pulled the covers up over her head.

Normally, she appeared between eight and nine for breakfast. It was a buffet style spread with yogurt, fresh fruit, rolls and coffee.

Sometimes Nico was there. Sometimes he wasn't. Today at ten, she heard a faint knock on her door. She groaned in reply.

The sound of keys clattering was her signal. She quickly gulped a glass she had tucked under the bedclothes, out of sight of the cameras. She had worked carefully to keep it upright under the covers. Keeping her head under the covers, she drank the syrupy sweet liquid, tucked the small juice glass under her pillow and pulled back the covers, squinting at the bright light as Esmeralda came to the side of the bed, peering down at her concerned.

Gabriella groaned. "I don't feel good."

"*Enferma?*"

"*Si*, sick."

The woman wrung her hands and looked around worriedly.

Gabriella leaned over and vomited on the floor beside the bed aiming for the small trashcan but missing and then feeling guilty that this woman would have to clean up her mess as part of her ruse.

The woman remained calm, gently holding back Gabriella's hair and wiping her face with a corner of her apron.

Gabriella gave her a weak smile of gratefulness. Ruse or not, she felt like shit.

And now this poor woman was nursing her.

But this guilt was a small price to pay. She had to stay focused on getting home and back to Grace.

Lying back weakly, Gabriella closed her eyes and listened to the sounds of the woman cleaning up the mess. When she was finally done mopping up the mess, she brought Gabriella a glass of water and set it on the nightstand, clucking sympathetically.

Again, Gabriella shot her a small smile, closed her eyes again and pretended to sleep until she heard Esmeralda leave, closing the door softly behind her. Listening carefully, Gabriella was relieved that she didn't hear the clatter of keys or the clock turning.

Now might be the hardest part. She would have to continue pretending to be sick, even taking more Ipecac later so she would continue her sporadic vomiting throughout the day. That way anyone watching her through the cameras wouldn't worry about her escaping tonight.

It would be easy to sleep all day. She didn't have to pretend. She was exhausted. She hadn't slept the night before.

And under the cover of darkness, she would take her new lock picking tools and open up the door to that office.

It was strange that Nico hadn't come to check on her. He must really be on to her now, which explained the locked doors and his sudden disappearance from her life.

But it might also help.

She wanted to avoid him so he didn't see the change in her, so that he didn't see suspicion in her eyes.

Sitting in front of the fireplace with him, she wouldn't be able to hide her sudden revulsion. She could fake small interactions, but she wouldn't be able to do enough of an acting job to convince him during their hours-long nightly rendezvous.

Getting sick, well, vomiting at least, was also designed to keep him far away.

One night, she'd quickly figured out he was a germaphobe, although he'd probably be mortified to know she thought of him that way. He had told a story about skipping a mission because he hadn't received the correct malaria shot in time and wasn't going to risk the trip. He said his superiors were extremely angry, but he drew the line on purposefully exposing himself to some foreign illness. He was so indignant about it, like it was normal to act that way.

It reminded Gabriella of the *mammonis*—Italian men who stayed unnaturally attached to their mothers and never really left that stage even as they grew into men in their thirties.

That's why she had also made dark circles under her eyes and left streaks of blood under her nose as if she had nosebleeds. It took cutting a small piece of her foot and bandaging it under a sock but she got enough blood to make it look real. She wanted him worried that she

had something much worse than just the stomach flu. The further away

he stayed, the better.

Tonight, after midnight, she would make her move.

CHAPTER THIRTY-SIX

After having slept most of the day, the first thing Gabriella did when she got up was turn off the lamp on her nightstand. Sometime after it grew dark, Esmeralda had drawn her blinds and turned on the small bedside light.

Now, in the dark, Gabriella kicked back her covers and did a series of stretches to work out her stiffness from lying in bed all day.

She quickly dressed in the dark, pulling on her trusty black cargo pants, a tank top, her jacket, and boots. She loaded her lock pick tools in her jacket pocket along with some items from the first aid kit-tiny scissors, bandages, antibacterial ointment and some antibiotic pills. Once again, she sent a silent prayer of thanks to her good friend photojournalist Chris Lopez for teaching her how to pick locks a few years ago.

The first step in her plan was to make a call on the office phone warning her mother and The Saint that her captors were coming for Grace once they found out she had escaped. Now that she had the right tools, the second step was to break into the garage and get the hell out of this place. She needed to get word to her mother that she was still alive. She needed to get home to see her mother before it was too late. If she had time, she would also try to get upstairs. If there were girls being held prisoner upstairs, she had to take them with her. She couldn't leave them behind. But then she realized that if there were other prisoners, the best way she could help them was to leave and get help.

She tugged her hair into a neat ponytail and plopped her baseball cap on before she crept toward her door. The squeaking wood of the floor seemed screamingly loud to her in the quiet of the dark. She tried her door handle.

It turned.

CHAPTER THIRTY-SEVEN

Gabriella pushed her door open as quietly as she could. She stuck her head out slowly, quickly glancing down the hall. It was empty. She listened but didn't hear anything so she stepped back into her room to pull her door closed. It would buy her some time if anyone passing by thought she was still asleep inside.

When she turned back, she froze.

A woman stood at the end of the long hall near where it led to the kitchen. Was this one of the women whose voices she had heard? But this woman was obviously not a prisoner.

Even from fourteen feet away in the dim light from sconces on the wall, Gabriella could tell the woman was stunning. She had a long sleek curtain of black hair that fell to her curvy waist and full pouty lips that were clearly bright red naturally. She wore a black flowing skirt and black embroidered peasant blouse that revealed a glimpse of a red satin bra and abundant cleavage. Her small bare feet with red painted toenails poked out the bottom of the skirt.

As soon as the woman saw Gabriella she half turned toward the kitchen, her mouth open as if she were going to scream or call for someone. But then she closed her mouth and turned back toward Gabriella, taking her in from her boot-clad feet to the baseball hat on her head. Gabriella calculated how long it would take to reach the woman and realized if the woman screamed or shouted, all bets were off. She held her breath waiting and watching to see what the woman was going to do. The faint scent of fresh bread came down the hall as if someone had opened a door somewhere letting in a breeze.

Clenching and unclenching her fists, Gabriella waited. For what must have only been seconds, but felt like an eternity, the two women stared at one another. Then, the woman nodded and looked down, turning away and slowly walked back into the kitchen.

Gabriella didn't wait around to see why the woman hadn't screamed or alerted anyone. Instead, she raced toward the door that led to the garage. Now that she'd been spotted, it was too risky to spend time picking the lock on the office door. She'd put her effort into breaking into the garage and trying to commandeer a vehicle. It was her best shot.

Racing by the office, she did pause long enough to turn the handle. It was locked as she suspected, so she continued running, bursting through the door to the outside and racing down the hill to the garages on the lower level.

Crouching down in front of the garage door, she took out her homemade lock pick tools.

Her hands trembled and she kept looking behind her and up the driveway, waiting for a gunman to appear and mow her down.

She slowed her breathing and tried to calm down so her hands would stop shaking and remain steady enough for her to do her job.

Within five minutes she had the lock undone. She ducked inside, closing and locking the door behind her. From the outside, nobody would know she had been able to break into the garage. In the dark, she could make out the shape of at least three vehicles.

Racing to each one—a Jeep, a sedan, and a truck—she checked the ignition and glove box for the keys. Nothing. Then she began searching the walls for a hook that might hold some keys. Nico had heard Esmeralda say the keys were kept in the garage, but she had no idea where they were.

In the dark, she relied on feeling her way along the walls. The keys had to be somewhere.

Outside she heard shouting and it made her heart race. They knew she'd left her room. The voices were just outside the garage now. She hid behind a vehicle in case someone could look through the tall widows at the top of the garage doors. After a moment, the voices seemed further away and she resumed looking for the vehicle keys.

She searched a small workbench with drawers, dumping each drawer out and feeling the contents. Her eyes had adjusted a little and she could make out more of the details of the garage by the light filtering in from the garage's three high windows.

She'd searched everywhere and was nearly sobbing with despair that she'd come so close to escaping. If Nico wasn't on her side, if he was the enemy, maybe he had lied when he told her they kept the keys in the garage with the vehicles.

Maybe it was all a lie, a trick to get her to think she could escape when she couldn't.

She willed herself to breathe in and out and gave herself a pep talk. Get your shit together. The keys have to be here somewhere. He wouldn't just make that up out of thin air.

She crawled into the Jeep and pulled down the visor. Nothing. Then she remembered how one of her uncles used to store a spare key under the floor mat on the driver's side. Racing to the Jeep, she dug her fingers under the mat and almost yelped when she felt a small piece of metal.

She hopped into the driver's seat, stuck the key in the ignition and with her other hand, got ready to press the small garage door opener button clipped to the driver's side visor.

Luckily the Jeep had been backed into the garage because as soon as that garage door opened, she planned to book out of there with the engine roaring. She'd wait until the door was barely open before she started the engine. Hitting the garage door opener, she cringed as it made a tiny squeak that seemed deafening to her ears in the quiet of the night. When there was only about five more feet until the garage door was all the way up, Gabriella turned the key in the ignition and made the sign of the cross.

The engine turned over.

She peeled out of the garage, burning rubber as she rounded the corner that led to the driveway. As she flew down the road, she could hear shouting behind her and then heard bullets hit the back of the Jeep at the same time the sound of gunshots reached her.

In the rearview mirror, she watched the figures of two men standing in the middle of the road firing at her.

Ducking down, she gripped the steering wheel tightly and took the corners as fast as she dared. She wasn't sure what she was going to do about the gates, ramming them probably wasn't an option. As soon as she was far enough away from the gunmen, she'd search the vehicle for any remote controls to operate the gate.

When they'd been brought in, the driver had been able to open the gate remotely.

Somewhere behind her she heard engines. Shit. They were

coming after her with the other two vehicles. At least the Jeep could go

off road if necessary. The truck and sedan would have a tougher time.

For a minute, she thought about taking it off-road, eyeing the jungle

around her, but she was pretty sure the fence surrounded the property.

Then she'd be a rat in a maze driving in circles with no way out.

Digging through the glove box revealed nothing. Then she saw

it. Clipped to the passenger side visor. The garage door opener had

been on the driver's side visor so she hadn't even glanced at the

passenger seat's one.

Just in time the first gate loomed before her down the hill. It

disappeared for a second as she took one of the last curves to reach it.

Punching the remote button, she waited, foot on the brake ready to

come to a skidding stop if the gate remained closed. She wondered how

hard it would be to scale the gate. But it would be impossible to survive

a trek through the jungle on foot. That became even clearer when she

rounded the corner and spotted two glowing eyes in the bushes at the

side of the road.

The gate swung open and she flew through, punching the

remote so the gate would close again behind her, possibly giving her a

few seconds head start when the people behind her had to open it again.

She still had the second gate at the bottom of the long winding drive. It was about five miles down, if she remembered correctly.

Racing down the road, she racked her brain to remember which way she should turn onto the road once she got there.

After a few heart pounding minutes, the gate came into sight and she punched the remote control. Nothing. She kept pressing it, not taking her eyes off the gate, keeping her foot pressing the gas pedal straight down. Finally, when she couldn't wait any longer, she slammed on the brakes skidding to a stop, dust kicking up everywhere. She nearly rolled the Jeep, which wobbled a little and then settled back on all four tires. When the dust cleared, to her surprise, she saw the gate swing open. Looking down at the road she saw she'd run over a cable that automatically opened the gate when a vehicle drove over it. It made sense. *El Loro* was more concerned with keeping people out than keeping people in.

Gunning the ignition and pressing the gas pedal down, she hung a right onto the main road. This felt like the direction they'd come from when they first arrived at the house. For a second, she let herself think of Nico back at the hacienda and felt a mixture of sadness, anger, and disappointment. If she were lucky, she'd never see him again. She'd developed feelings for the man. He didn't deserve them, but she couldn't help it.

But those feelings quickly faded. As the Jeep skittered around corners, bumping over the occasional large stick and pothole, Gabriella felt exhilaration. The cold night air was blowing her hair back around her and adrenaline was pumping through her limbs. She'd done it. She was away from the house. Now to get back to the airstrip or to a small town or outpost where she could call for help.

She listened over the sound of the engine for other vehicles, but she didn't hear anything. She kept glancing in the rearview mirror for lights, but there was nothing.

That's when she felt it—even before she heard it—a thumping vibration that sent goose bumps down her arms.

A helicopter.

CHAPTER THIRTY-EIGHT

The moment Donovan lunged for the gunman closest to him, a shout from the doorway above had the Italian man whirling and running up the stairs three at a time.

The door at the top of the stairs slammed shut, but Donovan didn't hear the lock slide into place.

Meanwhile, the gunman saw Donovan coming and swung the barrel wide. But it was too late. Grabbing the barrel of the automatic weapon, Donovan shoved, pushing the gun and the man behind it, off balance. For a few seconds the two men balanced precariously, scrambling to stay upright before they fell to the ground. They rolled on the ground, both clutching the gun that was between them. They knocked over the bucket, which was sent clattering. They rolled past the man who'd been bit by the spider, who was clutching his neck groaning, sweat pouring off his face onto the dirt floor.

Donovan continued wrestling for control of the gun, kicking and elbowing, yet joined to the man by his grip on the gun. He managed to avoid an incoming head butt, but both men slammed into the wall, smashing shoulders before falling on the ground, which clearly knocked the wind out of both of them.

Out of the corner of his eye, Donovan saw the second gunman crouching down to check on his spider-bitten comrade who was convulsing now.

Then the second gunman stood and aimed the gun Donovan's way. He was obviously a crack shot or didn't care about accidentally shooting his colleague because it looked like he was going to fire at the rolling mass of the two men.

Realizing he had only seconds to act, Donovan shifted and maneuvered himself underneath the other man. The man's look of surprise gave him another advantage. In one fluid motion, Donovan let go of the barrel and instead reached down, cupping the other man's hand on the trigger. Pressing on the other man's fingers with all his strength, Donovan squeezed off a few rounds. A barrage of deafening automatic gunfire was accompanied by the other man slumping to the ground, riddled with bullets.

Two down, one to go.

Taking advantage of having his arm in close to the man's body, Donovan elbowed the gunman in the face. The other man sunk to the ground, dazed but still conscious. But a few seconds later he scrambled toward Donovan tackling his legs so both of them were on the ground.

Within seconds both men were rolling around trying to gain control of the gun that was tangled between them. The gunman was gaining control. He was on top of Donovan about to bash him in the head with the butt of the gun when Donovan saw a threat he hadn't expected. The man who had been bit by the spider was crawling over to his gun. He watched as the man with the spider bite lifted his weapon, aiming it at Donovan's head.

At the last second, Donovan retrieved an old high school wrestling move and flipped the man on top of him. The bullet meant for Donovan exploded the other man's head, splattering brain and blood all over Donovan. Scrambling to get further away from the armed man, Donovan was halfway across the room when he realized that firing the gun had taken the last bit of life out of the other man. He was lying back with his eyes wide open staring at the ceiling.

Three men lay dead around him. Donovan eyed them all. One man was close to his build: the man bit by the spider, which was lucky since the other two men had bloodstained clothing. At one point, he spotted the spider high up on the wall by the window. It took a few minutes, but Donovan managed to get the khaki fatigues off the man and change into them. He then stripped all three guns off the dead men, slinging them onto his shoulder by their straps before he scaled the stairs.

CHAPTER THIRTY-NINE

Donovan tried the door at the top of the basement stairs.

Locked.

Even in his haste to leave, the Italian had managed to lock it.

Or else it was a door that automatically locked on closing.

Donovan thought back. He'd never heard the deadbolt slide shut. Maybe he could pick the lock. This made him instantly think of his wife.

Gabriella was part cat burglar with her lock picking skills.

Rushing back down the stairs, he searched the three bodies on the ground. The first one had a set of keys in his pants pocket.

Donovan fumbled with the keys at the door until he found one that fit. He turned it. The door opened.

He rushed out. He was in a long hallway with terra cotta floors and priceless art on the walls. He recognized a Degas and a Van Gogh. He was in some sort of large house, a hacienda. It was the first time he'd seen it since they'd kept him blindfolded during his one and only field trip out of the basement. Most of the doors were closed in the hallway. He was at the far end. He went through the first door he came to. It was a large kitchen. He went straight through to some French doors that led outside to a giant veranda. Glancing around him, he didn't know which way to turn or what to do.

The three guns he toted on his shoulder clanked loudly.

It seemed like the house was deserted. He started circling the veranda. On one side of the house was a deck area with lounge chairs and tables and further out, a giant pool on a plateau overlooking the jungle below. A tall stone wall seemed to surround the entire property.

As he neared the pool, Donovan recognized that the picture of Gabriella was taken in this exact spot. He ran over to the spot where she had lain on the chair, as if some trace of her might still be there. The realization nearly dropped him to his knees. Gabriella had been here, so close, the entire time?

That's when he felt her before he even saw her.

He turned.

Monica stood on the veranda watching him.

Her face was filled with sorrow. She looked down as she mouthed the words. "*Lo siento.*" I'm sorry.

CHAPTER FORTY

The Jeep skittered around a tight corner that had seemingly appeared out of nowhere. On the right side, two tires briefly left the ground. Gabriella was able to right the vehicle but not in time to avoid a large Tapir.

In her efforts to avoid the animal she swerved and the Jeep careened off the small lip of raised road and flipped in a giant cloud of dust.

Coughing, Gabriella realized the vehicle had landed on the passenger side and she was suspended by her seatbelt.

Unstrapping, she got out of the Jeep and surveyed the damage. If she could flip the Jeep back over, she could probably still drive it. She gave a few futile pushes to the side of the Jeep trying to right it. But her attempts only rocked the vehicle a little. Not enough to upright it. Gabriella looked around her frantically. The Jeep was useless. She leaned in and turned off the headlights in the hopes that *El Loro*'s men might drive right by it, but she knew that wouldn't happen.

In the distance, she heard the thump of the helicopter and her heart stopped for a moment until she realized the sound was moving farther away.

Without the Jeep, it would be a dangerous and long walk to the nearest village or any type of civilization. While this was considered a major highway in this area, it was still a deserted deep jungle road, which most people would avoid in the dead of night. She peered up at the sky peeking through the canopy.

A giant low-hanging full moon made it easy to see in the jungle, but even so, she could see the velvety sky beginning to turn purplish blue.

Morning was coming. Everything would be safer and easier by daylight. Maybe she could hide out in the jungle until morning. Off the ground would be better. She glanced around. Maybe she could find a tree to climb. It would at least give her a slight, albeit extremely slight, advantage if a jaguar came around. But the tree trunks were slick and she remembered the deadly spider that had dropped from a treetop onto her head. And didn't jaguars sleep in trees or something? Nowhere was truly safe.

The sound of engines made that clear. The noise was growing louder quickly. The Jeep wasn't far enough off the road. They would see it for sure. She took in the dense jungle, trying to decide what to do and where to hide. But when headlights rounded the corner, Gabriella

knew she only had one option.

She ran.

CHAPTER FORTY-ONE

Donovan grabbed Monica's arm so tightly she gasped.

"Where is she?"

When he noticed that she was biting back tears, he released his hold slightly but still didn't let go. The scent of her perfume was all he could smell. Once he had buried his face in her neck to inhale that scent. Now it made his stomach churn.

"She left," Monica whispered, looking around her. "A few minutes ago."

He heard a helicopter in the distance.

"Where are the others?"

"They went to look for her. Come." She put a finger to her lips and gestured for Donovan to follow her.

Donovan paused. Why should he trust her when she had been keeping him from his wife for months? He watched her long black skirt sweep the ground as she walked. She stopped and half turned, waiting. He pressed his lips together and started toward her.

She led him around the veranda, down some concrete steps and along a dirt path. As they rounded the corner, there was a small clearing on a level below the hacienda that was primarily taken up by a three-car garage with a terra cotta roof that matched the large house. All three of the large doors were open. The garage was empty.

Donovan grabbed her arm.

"Where did she go?"

Monica shrugged and shook her head. She gently uncurled his fingers from her arm and led him toward a small shed next to the garage. Taking a large circle of keys out of her skirt pocket, she knelt and quickly unlocked it. Inside were three motorcycles. She tossed Donovan a helmet and wheeled one of the bikes out. She reached out and placed the key in his palm, covering it with her hand.

Her eyes pleaded for forgiveness. She handed him a remote-control garage opener.

"For the gate."

Donovan searched her face for a moment. She was a victim, too. He couldn't blame her for what had happened. It was larger than both of them. He leaned down and gave her a soft kiss on the forehead.

"*Vaya con Dio,*" she said. Go with God.

Donovan started the motorcycle.

He was about to lift the kickstand, when Monica grabbed his arm.

"She ... she took the Jeep."

He was about to gun the motor but stopped and turned to Monica. "Will you be okay here? Are you safe?"

She nodded. He didn't know if he believed her, but he didn't have time to wait.

The bike kicked up gravel behind it in a fishtail as he took off down the driveway without a glance back. He opened the first gate with the remote-control Monica had handed him and then raced down the winding road that led deeper into the jungle. His hair blew back and his eyes watered.

When he got to the large gate at the foot of the property it was wide open. He came to a skidding stop trying to decide which way to go. Although the thick jungle canopy blocked most light, there was a tiny sliver of night sky visible. It seemed that the sky to the right was a little bit lighter than the black to the left. He usually had a good sense of direction and something told him that going to the right was the east and meant the coast, which is where Gabriella had probably headed.

CHAPTER FORTY-TWO

Branches and palm fronds tore at Gabriella's face, leaving bloody scratches that oozed down her cheeks as she ran. The ground was muddy and wet and she sometimes slid as she rounded corners, feeling the water seep into her boots.

Her breath was ragged; she tasted metal and felt as if her heart were going to explode. But she couldn't stop. The shouting behind her made that clear. The sound of a helicopter growing closer filled her heart with terror. The sky had lightened and was now a hazy gray blue above her. The jungle had come to life with the sounds of birds and insects. Even as she noisily tore through the trees and bushes, the cacophony didn't pause. The jungle creatures knew she was no threat.

In the distance, she heard a sound that sent a spike of fear through her. It was a large animal grunting and growling. A jaguar. Not close, thank God.

The sun was rising. She no longer had the cover of night to hide her from her pursuers. It didn't seem possible she could find her way out of this one.

Coming to a river, she looked both ways. It went as far as the eye could see. She shuddered before stomping through it, hoping it wasn't too deep. Hopefully her splashing would scare off any snakes or other creatures. Above in the trees, she heard the ominous snarling of the Howler monkeys, like a mammoth beast stalking her.

It seemed like they were calling for her captors, alerting them to her hiding spot. She felt something graze the top of her head and then splashing all around. The little shits were throwing some type of small fruit at her.

By the time she splashed to the other side, her thighs were soaked and something had struck her cheek, splattering something sticky along the side of her face. To top it off she felt something squishy on her elbow and plucked away a leech, leaving a bloody trail down her arm.

Now when she ran, the water squished in her boots, seeming to slow her path. She rounded a corner and there was another body of water. An estuary. If she followed it, it should lead her to the sea. At least she now had some sense of which way to run.

The clatter of the birds and monkeys overhead was deafening. She didn't know if her pursuers were close. If so, she'd never hear them coming.

That's why when Nico appeared out of the jungle suddenly in front of her, she screamed. He cut it off with a palm across her mouth. She began kicking him in the shins, stomping on the tender spot at the top of his foot where his ankle began. A move that had served her well in her karate class. This time it didn't work. When he twisted her arm behind her back, she stopped, howling in pain through his dry palm.

He leaned down in her ear.

"Stop fighting me. Come with me. I'm your only hope."

Her wild eyes met his. She shook her head.

"You have to trust me."

She stopped struggling.

"They are coming."

Voices and crashing in the distance convinced her. He let go of her mouth, waiting for her to scream. When she didn't, he grabbed her hand and ran, dragging her behind him.

She kept pace as they splashed across the estuary. He stopped, looked around and headed to the right, through some dense brush. Within seconds they were on a small dirt path that ran parallel to the estuary. The even ground was easier to run upon, but soon, they were both breathing heavily and loudly. Gabriella's mouth was dry. She was so thirsty, the thought of drinking out of the estuary seemed appealing.

"I have to stop and catch my breath," she said, panting.

He stopped and leaned down, palms on his knees. His hair fell into his eyes. He flipped it back and watched her, taking in her heaving chest.

She wanted to slap him but didn't have the energy. Instead she glared.

He surprised her by laughing.

But then his face grew somber and he straightened up, grabbing her hand.

"Come on, we're almost there."

CHAPTER FORTY-THREE

Holding Gabriella's hand, Nico stopped at a large tree. He examined the trunk for a minute and then led her off the dirt animal path and through thick bushes and trees. After about five minutes a small thatched hut came into view in a small clearing.

"Hurry." He ran ahead and moved aside a large board hung across the door. He held it open. "Inside."

For a second, Gabriella froze. Why should she trust him? Who knows what he'd do once he had her in an enclosed space. But then she saw the frightened look in his eyes as he glanced over her shoulder and knew he was on her side.

She ran inside and he quickly followed, pulling the door behind him.

The interior was dim with greenish light filtering through dirty windows. Gabriella was grateful for the chance to catch her breath and panted with her hands on her knees while she waited for Nico to say something. The damp interior of the hut sent a shiver through her and down her sweat-soaked body.

After a few seconds, she heard the spark of a match. Nico lit half a dozen candles that were on a small wood table. The light revealed a small room with a fireplace, cot with quilts pushed up against a wall and the small table. A crate nailed to one wall served as a pantry with several canned items. A small hot plate rested on the table.

"What is this place?"

"A safe house for drug runners. I saw it on a map in *El Loro*'s office."

Nico lifted the lid of a small chest tucked under the table. He pulled out a gallon of water. He opened it, took a slug, passed it to Gabriella and then pulled up a chair at the table.

Gabriella lifted the water bottle and gulped for several seconds before handing it back.

"Thanks."

Nico kicked out the other chair for her to sit, but she wasn't ready yet. She was still on guard, still ready to flee, still on high alert.

"Why are you helping me?" Gabriella asked.

He shook his head. "You really don't know?"

She didn't answer.

He gave a big sigh, his expression tough to see in the dim light. "I couldn't do it?"

"Do what?" She gritted the words.

"Betray you."

"What are you talking about?" She clenched her fists. The time for games was over.

"Don't you know?"

"Obviously not or I wouldn't be asking." She stood stock still, not taking her eyes off his.

"How I feel about you?"

She drew back.

He looked at her then and she saw it in his eyes, but she still said, "I don't believe you."

Nico shrugged.

Gabriella pulled up a chair and looked Nico right in the eye.

"Maybe if you start telling me the truth I'll believe something you say. Until then, as far as I'm concerned everything that comes out of your mouth is a lie."

He stared back for a second and then nodded. "Fair enough."

He leaned back and grimaced. "Shortly before we met in Guatemala, they kidnapped my son. His name is Alejandro. He is seven.

"They sent a message to me that I was to cooperate in making sure you ended up at *El Loro*'s ranch or my son would die. I, of course, agreed to whatever they said."

"Of course." Gabriella nodded reaching for the water bottle.

Nico paused then realized Gabriella was not being sarcastic.

"They wanted me to use you to find out if you knew the identity of the spy they are looking for."

"What spy?"

Nico shook his head.

"I never knew all the details. They let me talk to my son once a week to make sure he was okay."

Gabriella realized that when she'd caught him on the phone in the office, he'd been talking to his son's captors.

"Meanwhile," Nico continued. "My job was to keep an eye on you. To gain your trust to see if your husband had told you anything important before his plane crashed and he lost his memory. When you escaped this morning, I was given orders to kill you. But I couldn't do it. My feelings for you— "

"They wanted you to kill me?" Gabriella cut him off. She didn't want to hear about his feelings.

"Yes. But I am weak. I must get to my son. If they find out you live, I worry they will kill him."

"I don't understand," Gabriella stood so abruptly her chair tipped over. "Once you found out that I didn't know anything—that my husband hadn't told me anything about a spy—why was I kept alive?"

Nico closed his eyes.

It sent a shock of fear through Gabriella. "What? What aren't you telling me? Good God, what aren't you saying?"

Nico opened his mouth but the sound of a helicopter right above their heads drowned out anything he was about to say. Instead, he grabbed her hand and raced to the door. Along with the chopping sound of the helicopter, Gabriella heard popping noises and realized that small holes were appearing in the roof. They were being shot at. Nico tugged, pulling her out the door and into the jungle. Within seconds they were back in dense woods.

The helicopter hovered, but couldn't follow them into the dense jungle. It tracked their progress, staying as low as it could as they ran.

Nico held tight to her hand and began zigzagging through the trees. She understood why when she saw a bullet pierce a tree trunk beside them. Finally, they managed to go so deep into the jungle that the helicopter had to climb higher until it was above the canopy and couldn't get a clear shot of them.

Nico continued leading her, sometimes doubling back the way they came until the sound of the helicopter all but disappeared.

They ran until the jungle began to break up a little.

As they followed the winding path at times the shouting behind them grew louder, at times fainter.

Gabriella panted, unsure she could run anymore. Her legs and lungs ached. The only thing that kept her going was the image of hugging her mother and Grace.

CHAPTER FORTY-FOUR

They continued to run until they hit the estuary.

"We can follow this to the sea," Nico said as they paused to catch their breath. "It's the only way I know to get out of here. I'm very turned around now from trying to get away from the helicopter. What I do know is that the helicopter has notified everyone on the ground of where we are spotted. We don't have much time."

Gabriella was too out of breath to answer, so she just nodded.

They raced along the banks of the river for another ten minutes and then Gabriella heard an unfamiliar sound above the clattering and clamoring of the jungle noise.

An engine.

As the sound grew louder, Gabriella realized, too late, it was a boat.

It rounded the corner right when Nico pushed her down on the ground.

She collapsed in a heap, her mouth wide open with surprise.

"You bitch!" Nico shouted, his back to the boat, which had killed the engine and was gliding toward the shore. "You thought you could get away. You were wrong."

Gabriella saw the boat crawl closer. Two men inside pointed guns at them. Nico's eyes met hers. The message was clear: Play along.

"Fuck you," she shouted and tried to stand.

He put his foot on her and she acted as if he kicked her back down. All the while, she eyed the men in the boat. Meanwhile, Nico continued to scream at her.

"Tell us who the spy is?" he said. "This is your last chance. We have no more use for you. Tell us before you die?"

"I don't know what you're talking about," she cried, meaning every word.

Out of the corner of her eye, she saw the men moor the boat and hop onto the shore.

Nico very slowly reached into his jacket pocket and withdrew a handgun. Gabriella, who was on her knees, shrunk back in horror.

The men were right behind Nico now and said something in Spanish. He nodded and replied in a clipped voice. He reached down, the gun pointing toward her forehead. It seemed he was about to shoot her when he whirled and in two quick bursts shot the men behind him. The first right in the face, the second in the neck. Both men toppled.

As they fell, she caught sight of a third gunman who had crept up on the path behind them. The man reached for his gun. In seemingly slow motion, Gabriella watched as he held it up, pointing directly at her. Their eyes met as he squeezed the trigger. All she could see was the man's eyes and the gun. Before she could hear the blast, the man disappeared, Nico's body thrust between them. The blast of the gun sent him flying backward. He landed in her lap. She heard more gunshots but didn't even look up.

Instead, she held Nico.

"My son." Nico said closing his eyes for a second as if wincing in pain.

He tried to sit up and clutched at her hands. Gabriella could tell he was growing weaker. His grip was fading on her hands.

She squeezed his hand. "We'll get your son. We'll find him."

"Promise me you will take care of him."

"I don't know if I can promise that." Without looking up, she heard voices nearby. She was not going to look away from Nico in his last few seconds, even if it meant a bullet to her head. This was all she had to give him—some measure of comfort during his last moments of life.

He gave the slightest nod.

She squeezed his hand again. "I promise I will try."

Nico's eyes met hers and he smiled right before the light left them.

Her vision became blurry with tears. She was half in shock, half exhausted. She couldn't run anymore. If they killed her now, that was how it was supposed to be. She didn't have any more fight in her. This man had just died in her arms. For her. She held him until she noticed somebody standing over her.

As the shadow fell across Nico's face, she looked up, expecting to meet her death.

What she saw sent her reeling.

Donovan.

He was alive. She started to get up, words strangled in her throat, but something stopped her. It was the look on his face—a potent mixture of rage and love and disgust.

She knew him like she knew herself. Immediately she knew he was taking in the scene before him and it was breaking his heart. She was weeping and tenderly holding another man. A dead man, but a man she had made love to. Donovan looked at her as if he knew all of this in a glance.

So many emotions ran through her—ecstatic joy and shock that Donovan was alive, shame that she was a married woman and yet felt love for the dead man in her arms, and horror that Nico had died for

her.

CHAPTER FORTY-FIVE

Donovan felt stiff in Gabriella's arms. She was hugging him as if she'd never let go and he was barely responding. She wondered what he had seen and gone through to make him this way. Maybe he'd been tortured and had suffered psychological damage. Whatever it was, she'd be there to help him through it.

All around them in the deep jungle, seemingly from out of nowhere, a half dozen men in black pants and tee-shirts appeared, talking on radios, covering up bodies and picking up fallen tree branches in a nearby clearing to make way for a helicopter that was landing to pick them up. They were speaking English. They were American.

Finally, they were being rescued. But Gabriella only took it in distantly—she couldn't take her eyes off Donovan.

"I thought you were dead," she said.

He scowled as if he didn't believe her.

"They told us that." She swallowed. Why did she have to justify herself? He turned away frowning.

"Who told you that?"

"The DEA."

He whirled, his face suddenly filled with horror. "Does Grace think that? That I'm dead?"

Gabriella nodded, fighting back tears. "She thinks I'm dead, too."

Donovan stormed off and grabbed one of the men in black by the collar of his shirt, almost lifting him up from the ground.

"Who the fuck is in charge around here? Get me a satellite phone now before I break some motherfucking heads in."

Gabriella rushed over and put her hand on his arm. "It's not their fault, Sean."

He shook her hand off, glared at her, opened his mouth as if to say something and then closed his lips together and stormed into the clearing where he began throwing logs around helping the other men.

It was going to take some time. Whatever had happened over the past three months was not going to just disappear in a few moments.

She looked back at Nico's body. Instead of seeing his dark hair and long black eyelashes resting on his cheeks, he was now a lifeless lump inside a black plastic body bag.

CHAPTER FORTY-SIX

Although Gabriella didn't want to let Donovan out of her reach, he sat across from her in the military helicopter. He looked away every time her eyes met his.

Gabriella's stomach felt like acid.

Soldiers of some sort surrounded them. The sound inside the chopper was deafening, so even if she'd wanted to talk to him, it would have been difficult.

After a few minutes of avoiding her gaze, Donovan leaned his head back against the metal interior and closed his eyes.

Gabriella's uneasiness turned to fear. Her husband was alive. He sat there right in front of her, but the Donovan she knew was nowhere around. That man was gone. She just hoped that she could bring that man back again.

When they landed and disembarked, Donovan walked ahead without a backward glance. She caught up and put her hand in his, squeezing. He didn't brush her hand away. So far so good.

They were inside a military camp. The area was still in the jungle but surrounded by barbed wire fences with camouflage netting strung on them. She'd seen as they landed that the few squat beige

buildings also had camouflage netting on their roofs.

A man in a beige uniform stood in front of one of the buildings,

his hands clasped behind his back until they got closer. He stepped

forward and stuck his hand out for Donovan to shake.

"Colonel Ryan Runge."

"Nice to meet you, sir."

"We're relieved to find you alive, Special Agent Donovan."

Donovan nodded.

Runge peered behind him. "Mrs. Donovan."

Gabriella didn't bother correcting him, but Donovan spoke up.

"Mrs. Giovanni."

The colonel looked from one to the other and nodded. "My

apologies."

Gabriella felt a small flicker of anger light deep inside her. She

knew Donovan had basically been a prisoner of war—a drug war—but

that didn't mean she was going to let him treat her like shit.

She stepped forward.

"My husband has been through a lot, sir." She put on her most

charming smile. "If you don't mind terribly, can we get this started

with so we can get home to our daughter and my mother? As you might

imagine, we are both worried sick about them."

Donovan shot her a glance, raising an eyebrow. He didn't even know her mother was dying.

"We need to call her. Right now she thinks her mother and father are dead. I'm not talking to anyone until I talk to my daughter and my mother."

She hoped what she said was true. Her mother had to still be alive. She refused to accept any other alternative.

For a second the man paused but then nodded. "Understood. This way please."

They went into a small office that was bare except a desk, chairs and a filing cabinet. No pictures or personal items. Runge dialed some numbers and pushed the satellite phone's receiver toward Donovan.

He reached for it and then his hand paused above it. He turned to Gabriella. "I think you need to start first."

Gabriella nodded and grabbed the phone. When she heard her mother's voice answer the phone, she burst into tears.

"Mama? Oh my God, mama," she couldn't speak for a second.

"*Dios mio.* Gabriella? We've been waiting to hear from you. They told us you were alive." Who had called her? And when?

"Mama, are you okay?"

"Of course." Her mother's voice was no nonsense.

Gabriella took a deep breath. "We found him. Donovan. He's alive."

For a few seconds it was completely silent. Then, Maria choked out her words, *"Grazie al Signore."*

Her mother was then quickly apologizing. "They found your daddy, he's alive, Grace. He's alive."

Gabriella's face was wet with tears. She didn't bother wiping them away and they dripped into her lap.

"Mama?" It was Grace's little voice. "You and daddy are alive?"

"Yes," Gabriella chocked out the word. "Do you want to talk to him?"

She didn't wait for her daughter to answer. Wordlessly, Gabriella handed Donovan the receiver.

Tears were streaming down his face. She handed him the phone and he reached for her with his other arm, wrapping her in his arms, pressing her face to his shirt.

It was going to be okay. They'd survive this like they'd survived everything else they'd been through.

CHAPTER FORTY-SEVEN

Shortly after they spoke to Grace, Donovan and Gabriella were taken to separate areas to shower and dress in clean clothes. The khaki military fatigues were baggy on Gabriella, but at least they were clean—not seeped in Nico's blood.

Waiting in the small room by the clothes was a peanut butter and jelly sandwich and potato chips. Gabriella ate them in less than two minutes.

Then a soldier knocked on her door. Donovan stood behind him in similar clothes to hers. His hair was wet. He had a small speck of peanut butter near his lip that she gently wiped away, but he seemed to draw back from her touch. He walked ahead, catching up to the solider leading them back to Col. Runge's office. Two men she didn't recognize were already waiting in the office chairs. One man, wearing a nondescript navy pinstriped suit and light blue tie, stood and held out his hand.

"Owen Jackson from the American embassy in Mexico City."

Gabriella shook his hand then shot a look at the second man who remained seated and was watching her. He also wore a suit, a black one with a black shirt and black tie. His hair was longer and slicked back. His shoes reflected the light bulb hanging in the ceiling above. Something told her she should know who this man was, but she didn't.

The colonel ignored the other man, as well.

"I'm sure you have some questions," he said, gesturing for them to sit.

As they paused in the doorway, Gabriella tried to meet Donovan's eyes, but he looked away. She tried to reassure herself that her husband was traumatized and it would take time for things to return to normal. She reached out to squeeze his hand, but it was limp and unresponsive and she soon let it go.

She sat on the love seat against the window, hoping Donovan would sit beside her, but he pulled out a chair in front of the desk.

"Damn right. I need some answers," Donovan said as soon as they settled in.

"It looks like *El Loro* wasn't really after you."

"No shit," Donovan said. The colonel ignored the interruption and continued.

"There was someone on your plane. A Colombian that purported to be your guide. Do you recall him?"

Gabriella watched Donovan's face carefully. He squinted and nodded.

"Yes. Short fellow. Didn't talk much."

The colonel nodded back. "That was Carlos Ruiz Domingo Gonzales. He is head of the Belize Secret Service. There is a hefty reward for his capture. Alive."

"Why?" Gabriella was now leaning forward listening.

"He has two crucial bits of information that *El Loro* wants. He knows the identity of a key informant high up in the ranks of the cartel."

"Anyone want to bother explaining why this guy was on my plane?" Donovan said.

The other man cleared his throat. "He was picking up one last piece of intelligence before we were going to smuggle him out of the country so he could testify against *El Loro*."

Donovan raised an eyebrow, waiting.

The colonel pressed his lips together tightly before answering. "He was on his way to *El Loro*'s house to get a disk that contained proof that an official in our government has been compromised."

"An official? How high up?" Gabriella's reporter instincts kicked in.

"I'm sorry that's classified."

"That's bullshit," Donovan said standing. "I've spent the last four months in a basement while my family—my daughter—thought I was dead. My wife was kidnapped, leaving our daughter to believe she was orphaned.

"With the hell our family has gone through you damn well better tell me everything. I don't give a shit if it's classified or not."

The two men exchanged looks. The Colonel said, "My sources say it's going to be on the cover of the *Washington Post* in the morning."

The other man nodded.

"Senator Corbin has been receiving payments from *El Loro* for the past two years. In return, he overlooks intelligence he receives privately about *El Loro*'s covert drug operations. We did not know this until now. In other words, our work here has been completely useless and compromised."

"What?" Gabriella was exhausted. Nothing was making sense.

The senator was corrupt. He'd sold her out. Gabriella tried to keep her fury at bay to listen to what else the colonel had to say.

"Unfortunately, someone tipped Corbin off that we were on to him. Corbin put out a hit on Gonzalez to make sure that proof of his involvement never reached the Oval Office. That's why Donovan's plane was shot down."

Gabriella froze. Donovan's plane was shot down. It didn't have engine trouble and crash. She watched Donovan. He didn't react. He was concentrating on what the colonel was saying.

"Unfortunately for Corbin," the colonel said. "Gonzalez disappeared with the plane crash. His body was never found. Corbin feared he had survived the crash and was still going to expose Corbin's involvement and also provide the proof the government needed to charge *El Loro* in international court. They were holding Donovan to try to find out more about Gonzalez. Your memory loss, Agent Donovan, was inconvenient to them, but you were the only lead they had. Everyone else in the plane crash died. Except for you and Gonzalez. They found you, but not him. But while you were passed out, they found a note from Gonzalez on your body. It said that no matter how much they tortured you, he pleaded with you not to reveal his whereabouts."

"Son of a bitch." Donovan stood.

"Yes," the colonel said. "It was a set up. To lead them astray. Lucky for you, you had memory loss so they were waiting for your memory to return before any real torture took place."

Donovan sank back down into his chair. "What about my wife? God damn it. What about her? What did she have to do with this?"

The colonel turned toward Gabriella now.

"When you went to Corbin and told him you were going to search for Donovan, you played right into his hands. They thought by holding you, they would have all the power over your husband they needed to get him to reveal Gonzalez's location."

Gabriella closed her eyes for a second. They'd been fucking pawns in a deadly game they knew nothing about. Her so-called friend, the senator, had set her up and nearly killed her husband. He'd encouraged her to trace Donovan's path so he could use her to get Donovan to tell them everything he knew. Her eyes narrowed. Sen. Corbin would pay for what he had done to her family.

"How does all this tie into the Bay Area?" she asked.

The colonel nodded at Donovan. "Why don't you tell her what the DEA was investigating?"

"San Francisco is *El Loro*'s main conduit for distributing cocaine," Donovan said. "Those bodies in Lake Josephine were drug mules. Young women who thought they were starting exciting lives in America. But instead something went wrong. For this particular group of women, the balloons they had swallowed with the drugs were old, had sat in the sun too long and burst inside them, killing them instantly. Lake Josephine wasn't a secret spot where bodies were occasionally dumped. It was the burial ground after a mass execution. An accidental execution, but still. *El Loro* knew—and wanted—the bodies to surface to send a message. Each body had a parrot's feather in its mouth."

Gabriella frowned.

"*El Loro* means "the Parrot" in Spanish," Donovan said. "My mission was to find him and bring him into custody for the deaths of those young women and make sure the smuggling operation stopped. Forever.

"Obviously, I failed." He looked down.

"No, you didn't." Gabriella turned to the colonel. "What happened to the young women at the hacienda? Did you find them? Rescue them?"

The colonel nodded. "They are all in protective custody."

Gabriella gave Donovan a knowing look, but he wouldn't meet her eyes.

"Your 'tipster' who called the newsroom about the bodies was one of *El Loro*'s operatives," the colonel continued. Not noticing the exchange between the other two. "It seems that the bodies hadn't surfaced on their own so they alerted the media."

"Why me?"

"They also called the San Francisco paper, but some intern ignored it, figuring it was some crazy person."

"What now? What happens without that proof against Corbin and *El Loro*?" she said.

"Well, that's where we've had a bit of luck. Although Gonzalez's whereabouts are unknown, we received an email yesterday from a computer at *El Loro*'s home office with all the proof we need."

Nico.

It was if the colonel read her mind. "Nico Sicilia sent it."

CHAPTER FORTY-EIGHT

Hours later, after extensive questioning and repeating their stories—at least the bare bones of their stories—the men left Donovan and Gabriella alone for a few minutes. It was the first time they'd been alone for six months.

Gabriella was still reeling from the account Donovan gave of his captivity. Both were in disbelief that they had been so close for so long.

When the door closed behind them, Gabriella stared at the floor, suffused with guilt. She had made love to another man with her husband in the same house, alive. He was being held in a dingy basement prison without sunlight below her, maybe even directly below her bed, while she flirted and drank wine with another man and then kissed every inch of his body.

Gabriella didn't know how she was going to tell him or how they would ever recover from this.

But it was as if Donovan already knew. Besides those moments when he softened while talking to Grace on the phone, everything about him was stiff and cold. He knew her so well maybe he already did know that she had betrayed him.

Well, if not, he would know soon. She couldn't live with herself if she didn't tell him.

She stared at Donovan, willing him to look at her.

Instead, he reached forward and slid a manila folder off the colonel's desk. The tab had a small typed label that read, "Sean Donovan/Gabriella Giovanni."

Setting it casually in his lap, he opened it up. A stack of pictures was on top of a thick bundle of other papers. He stared at three photos that had splayed across the page when he had moved the folder. Gabriella leaned forward to see them and then felt sick.

They were pictures of her. In her bikini. In an evening gown, cheeks flushed with wine and a sultry smile on her mouth, clearly directed toward a man just out of the camera's range. She lay beneath a man's naked body. A man who was clearly not Donovan.

"Donovan," she reached for his arm.

He brushed her arm away, not roughly but firmly. "I've already seen these." His voice was dull, emotionless.

"I don't understand."

"They showed them to me when I was in the basement."

"I thought you were dead. I'm sorrier than I can ever say."

There was nothing else to say.

But then she spotted the corner of another picture. This was a different woman's face. Donovan didn't move as Gabriella leaned over and plucked the photo out. Her face felt numb. It was Donovan and the woman she'd seen in the hall last night. Having sex.

Leaning over, she grabbed the stack of photos. There were half a dozen similar pictures. In each one, the woman was half dressed in different outfits, so it was clear they were different times.

Stunned, Gabriella sat back in her chair, staring at the wall in front of her.

Donovan didn't move, didn't speak.

Finally, Gabriella said without looking away from the wall, "At least I only fucked him once."

Outside the office, the sounds of the jungle awakening for the night grew louder: the squawking of the parrots and chatter of the monkeys and far in the distant, the howl of something ominous and predatory.

The door opened and the colonel returned.

"We have a lead on *Senor* Sicilia's boy. *El Loro* owned at least a dozen homes in this area that we know about, but there is one we learned about from your friend," here he looked at Donovan. "She said he kept it secret. It is on the coast. We will go there."

Your friend. Gabriella's stomach flipped at the words. She wanted to squeeze her bare hands around that woman's neck until that pretty face became blue. With a start, she realized it wasn't the woman's fault. It was Donovan's. He was the one who betrayed her. The woman was innocent. In fact, the woman had helped Gabriella and was now helping authorities. She had probably been this *El Loro*'s prisoner, in many ways, as well.

Nobody was completely innocent in this fucked-up situation and yet, nobody was completely guilty. It was all shades of gray.

"Excuse me, colonel," Gabriella said. "Can you tell me where you got the photos in that folder?"

The colonel's neck turned red. He swallowed before he answered. "They were on Nico Sicilia."

Gabriella didn't answer. The phone rang. Donovan sat rigidly beside her.

The colonel spoke for a few minutes in a low voice before hanging up and meeting Gabriella's eyes.

"We are infiltrating the beach house at midnight. The woman knows a secret way in. We're taking her with us."

"What will happen to the boy?" Gabriella asked.

"We'll bring him here."

"Good." Gabriella stood up and without looking at Donovan said, "I made a promise to his father. I will take care of him."

\#

The call came at three in the morning. The colonel, who was still sitting at his desk, took the call.

Gabriella had dozed off on a small loveseat in the corner, covered with a blanket but sat up straight when the phone rang. Donovan was slumped in the chair. He straightened with a jolt.

They'd found the boy. Five people had died. They'd found him in a bedroom that had a flat screen TV and video games and books and Legos. He'd been treated well. Physically.

Emotionally, he was a mess, the colonel said.

"There is more," the colonel said. "Our men raided a small cave near a narco ranch one hundred miles north of here."

Gabriella waited darting a glance at Donovan.

"We think they found Gonzales. They found his body or a body they think is he. They only found parts," the colonel paused, as if debating to describe what parts and then continued. "He was in a small cave inhabited by hundreds of dart frogs. We might do an autopsy, but it won't matter. Animals had eaten him. He's been dead for a long time. Maybe shortly after the plane crash."

"Why won't an autopsy matter? What if he was murdered and stashed in that cave? He doesn't get any justice? Too bad? Jungle vigilance?" Gabriella was pissed and she didn't know why. She could care less about this Gonzales guy who had made her life hell the past few months.

"We shall see about the autopsy," the colonel said. "But personally, I believe he died from poisoning. He sought shelter in the wrong cave. The Golden Poison frogs found in the cave have enough venom on their skin to kill a man who simply touches one, especially a man with open cuts and wounds from a plane crash."

Gabriella knew then why she was furious: The whole time they'd been torturing Donovan and keeping Gabriella in the hopes that he might know the man's location, the man had been dead in a mountain cave. He hadn't been a threat at all.

It was almost too much to take in. Gabriella felt sick to her stomach and glanced around for some type of container in case she couldn't keep it down.

They had been drinking coffee and eating small sandwiches, waiting for word of the raid at the beach house and now all she could taste was the sour remains of her snack trying to fill her mouth.

But the colonel wasn't done. A third operation was taking place: a hunt for *El Loro*. When they'd raided the hacienda, there was not a trace of him. Only the young women.

They hadn't heard any word yet of how that hunt was going, he said.

"I know this is a lot to take in and it is all happening very quickly," the colonel said, standing. "Try to get a little sleep before we leave. A driver will be here at eight to take you to the air strip."

He told them they'd have to stop in Mexico City to go through some paperwork at the American Embassy there.

"I will leave you now to rest."

Gabriella leaned her head back and fell asleep.

When she woke at six, Donovan wasn't in the room. She opened the door and found a man outside with a gun.

"Where is the colonel?"

"Sleep."

"Did the boy get here?"

"*Si*, he is there." The man pointed at another door across the hall. Gabriella peeked in. The boy was curled up on a cot in a tiny office. A beige blanket covered his midsection. His legs stuck out the bottom. He still wore small buckled leather sandals. He looked so small and vulnerable. And now, he was an orphan. Her heart went out to him.

After using the bathroom, she returned to the colonel's office. The man who had been posted outside the door was gone. Inside, the colonel sat at his desk, looking as if he'd had a full night's sleep, hair slicked back, uniform unwrinkled. Donovan sat in the corner with messy hair and a three-day beard. She wanted to rush over to him and hold him. She wanted him to hold her and tell her everything would be okay, but right now he felt like a stranger.

Looking at him, her mind knew it was her husband, but her body told her that man was someone she'd never met.

For a second, she hesitated, waiting for him to meet her eyes so she could see the love in them, but when he looked up his eyes were blank, as if she were a stranger who meant nothing to him one way or the other.

CHAPTER FORTY-NINE

Gabriella knocked on the office door.

"*Si*, come in." The boy's voice was barely a whisper.

Inside the boy sat on the side of the cot, swinging his legs. A chunk of his hair stuck up and he tried to smooth it down when he saw Gabriella.

"*Mi chiamo es* Gabriella," she said.

The boy looked relieved she was speaking Italian.

She told him she was here to help him. He didn't answer, but she saw his little Adam's apple bob. He was nervous. When she asked if he spoke English he said he did, but not well.

"Well, you are going to come with me to America until we figure out the best place for you. Is that okay? I know this must be terribly frightening and sad."

He looked down as she said this.

"I knew your father and I know he loved you more than anything else in the world. You were his life. I know that for sure."

The boy nodded staring at his sandals.

"I will do everything I can to make this comfortable for you. Please don't hesitate to come to me and let me know anything you need or want. I am here to help you."

She paused. What else could she say? The boy was now alone in the world.

I'm so sorry." She left the room before he could see her tears.

#

Before they left for the airstrip, the colonel received another call.

"Yes, sir. Yes, sir. I see. Understood. Thank you, sir."

He hung up and leaned back in his chair.

"It seems that things have taken a new direction."

El Loro had been arrested trying to board a private jet he kept at an airport in the southern part of the country. Eight people died in the attempt to capture them.

Which reminded Gabriella of the gunfight at *El Loro*'s hacienda. She asked the colonel about it.

"We lost three special forces operatives that day. We'd heard from your father-in-law that you and Agent Donovan might be prisoners of *El Loro*. We sent three different teams to three of *El Loro*'s homes to see if we could find you. That particular operation was the one that went the most south. We didn't lose anyone in the other two raids. They weren't heavily guarded like the hacienda. We had to high

tail it out of there before we lost more men. The sheer number of men

he had responding to our raid showed us two things—Sen. Corbin

tipped him off, and that he was trying to hide something important at

that location. In fact, if our surveillance hadn't picked up on your

escape yesterday, we had plans to enact another raid, this one with

more manpower and firepower, tomorrow night."

Gabriella listened carefully to everything the colonel said and

then asked, "Can we please go home now?"

He nodded. "We leave for the airstrip in ten minutes."

They headed down the hall. Donovan was bringing up the rear,

so Gabriella held back. She stopped by Donovan. His face was blank,

but she knew he was in pain.

"Donovan, I'm sorry that this happened to us."

She reached for his hand and he jerked away. That did it. She

was tired of feeling like the only one who had done something wrong.

Hurrying, she caught up to him. She leaned over as she passed and said.

"At least when I had sex with someone else, it's because I thought you

were dead."

She rushed up to the boy and put her arm around him as they

walked to the Jeep.

The colonel said goodbye to them in the driveway. A soldier took the wheel. Donovan sat in the passenger seat. Gabriella and the boy got into the second row. It was quiet as they drove the winding roads to the airstrip.

Rounding one corner, Gabriella saw something out of the corner of her eye. It was an old woman standing at the edge of the jungle, staring at their vehicle. The woman had long gray hair that hung loose and a beige dress. She lifted a gnarled finger and pointed at Gabriella sending a chill down Gabriella's spine. She quickly looked beside her at the boy. He was looking out the other window, Gabriella saw and was filled with relief. When Gabriella turned back, the woman was gone, as if she'd never been there or as if Gabriella had imagined her presence.

Gabriella didn't know exactly what she had seen, but she knew enough to realize that it was a bad omen.

CHAPTER FIFTY

It was the first time Donovan had stepped foot in a plane since his crash.

They were taking the smaller plane to Mexico City where they would board The Saint's private jet to San Francisco.

Gabriella watched Donovan buckle in, on alert for any signs of stress, such as his neck muscles tightening or nervous clenching of his jaw. But Donovan's whole body oozed weariness and despair.

She knew it was because of her. She regretted her harsh words earlier, but she was pissed. It wasn't fair that he was acting like he was the only wounded one here. He was acting like he had done nothing wrong. They both had fucked up. And big time. But both of them had extenuating circumstances. And even though she was furious with him right now, she also felt overwhelming relief and joy that he was actually alive. She'd give him time to cool off and then try again. She wouldn't let him get away that easy. Not after losing him once. She was determined to make it work. They'd get over this. They had to.

As the plane taxied down the runway Donovan had his head turned away, staring out the small rectangular plane window. Gabriella reached out to stroke his arm, but drew her hand back before she touched his sleeve.

Instead, she leaned forward to peer out Donovan's window.

The jungle surrounding the runway was dense and shadowy, a ruthless opponent for man and a sanctuary for predators and secrets as old as the earth itself. A sky dark with clouds had made the day even more ominous than usual.

The faster the plane went, the more the trees blurred into one solid mass of darkness. Gabriella shivered as the plane's speed accelerated, clutching her miraculous medal and closing her eyes until she felt the nose lift into the air.

Seeing the crone on the way to the airport filled Gabriella with an ancient sense of foreboding. She couldn't help but think that the crone was the jungle in human form and that the jungle was not going to let them leave this easily. She closed her eyes and said a small prayer.

When she opened her eyes, she was startled to find Donovan staring at her with an inscrutable look.

She swallowed and looked away, out her window. As the plane made a swooping turn, suddenly the jungle canopy filled her window. It was all she could see until a few minutes later when they crept into the thick cloud cover and everything became white.

When she turned back, Donovan was staring at her again. It looked like he was about to say something when they heard a small sound from behind them.

It was the boy waking up.

When Gabriella unbuckled her seatbelt, Donovan closed his mouth and turned away toward his window.

Gabriella settled into the seat beside Alejandro. And stroked his hair. He'd had a bad nightmare. She gently murmured the few comforting words of Italian she knew. *Partecipo al tuo dolore* – I share in your sadness and *povero bambino*- Poor baby. She stroked his hair until he closed his eyes again.

Outside the window, it grew even darker and pellets of rain started pelting the small window. The plane rocked from side to side, buffeted by the storm like a kite. The boy's head rocked a little on the seat with the movement, but she could hear the sounds of his deep sleep. She clutched the armrests of the small plane, closing her eyes and praying for their safe trip home.

Lightning flashed and she caught a glimpse of Donovan's face in the seat in front of her. She didn't recognize the once familiar contours of his face, his cut jaw and cheekbones and heavy brows. He looked like a stranger. His obvious pain and fury made his face

unfamiliar and seemingly distorted. Clearly, whatever he was thinking

was dark and vicious and ugly. It was all over his face. A trickle of

dread crept down Gabriella's spine.

That's when she realized. She'd gotten it all wrong. The jungle

may have let them go, but it was not done with them yet. Not by a long

shot.

CHAPTER FIFTY-ONE

In Mexico City, they boarded a private jet the Saint had sent for them. Gabriella curled up in a lounge-type seat and slept for much of the flight. Alejandro sat beside her. She tried to hold his hand but he pulled it away giving her a sad look. Too soon. She was a stranger to him.

Donovan had sat toward the back of the plane. Every time Gabriella turned to meet his eye, he looked out the window. It was as if it were too painful to even look at her.

It was going to take some time. There were too many emotions in the space between them right now.

Meanwhile, Gabriella was sick with worry about her mother. The Saint had said she was too weak to meet them at the airport, but they would go directly to see her.

When the plane landed in San Francisco and Gabriella saw The Saint's limousine waiting, she gently guided Alejandro toward it, trying not to hurry in her eagerness to see her mother.

When she reached The Saint, he gave her a smile of such sorrow she thought for a moment her mother had passed, but then he said, "Your mother is very excited to see you. Let's not waste any time."

"How is she?"

The Saint's face grew dark. "She's hanging in there."

Donovan's face crinkled. Gabriella was too exhausted to do anything but give him the cold, hard facts. "My mom is dying of breast cancer."

He opened his mouth as if to speak, but then clamped his lips together. Instead, he surprised her by reaching over and enveloping her in a hug. With her face pressed to his chest, she fought back tears. He kissed the top of her head and then drew away.

There was a moment of silence and then, to her surprise, the Saint launched into perfect Spanish. He said something that made the boy laugh.

It was the first time she'd seen the boy even smile. She couldn't help but smile, too. This poor kid, all alone in the world, dropped suddenly in a foreign country. She vowed right then to do whatever she could to make him feel comfortable and welcome and wanted.

They piled in the back of the limousine. She and Donovan sat across from The Saint and Alejandro. Donovan immediately poured a tall glass of bourbon, downed it and poured another.

She nudged him aside and filled her own glass and did the same. He nodded at her wryly.

Across from them, The Saint was showing Alejandro various buttons and what they would do: opening the sunroof, lowering the dark window between the backseat and the front and turning on a small TV.

The cars and lights and sounds were overwhelming after months in the jungle. She wondered if the boy felt the same. But he arched his neck to see out. At one point, The Saint pulled out a small stool and the boy stood on it, his head and neck sticking out the top of the sunroof, taking in his first view of San Francisco.

She glanced at Donovan, staring out the limousine window at the cityscape. He was angry right now, but he wasn't coldhearted. Somewhere in there her Donovan still lived beneath the layers of pain and betrayal. He would come around.

CHAPTER FIFTY-TWO

When they arrived at the penthouse, Gabriella rushed inside and found Maria propped up on Gabriella's couch with a velvety pink blanket over her lap. Grace was beside her, holding her hand as they watched 'Cinema Paradiso." It was near the end of the movie and they both had tears streaking their faces. The movie was too old for Grace, but Gabriella didn't say a word.

Gabriella leaned over and gathered her mother and daughter in her arms, hugging them. Grace was crying and laughing all at once. She kissed her mother and then when she saw Donovan standing in the doorway, she shrieked and ran over to him, hugging his legs and laughing and crying.

Gabriella watched with a smile and then turned back to her mother, who felt so frail in her arms. Her mother patted Gabriella's back and whispered in her ear, "You're going to be just fine. I know it."

Gabriella bit back tears. She would not cry. Her goal in life was to be strong so her mother didn't worry about her. Her mother looked over Gabriella's shoulder at Donovan.

"Get over here right now, Sean!"

Not letting go of Grace's hand, he walked over with a huge grin, which startled Gabriella. She hadn't seen him smile since they were reunited. But his smile was genuine for Maria. He loved her. He knelt down and gave her a hug and a tickle that had her laughing and protesting.

"Thank God you both are alive," Maria said once he pulled back. "The Lord is good. He answered my prayers. It's a miracle."

Sneaking a glance at her husband, Gabriella thought it didn't feel like a miracle to her right then. But she smiled back at her mother.

Then Maria noticed Alejandro, who was hanging back in the doorway. The Saint must have filled her in on the phone earlier because she greeted him with a large smile.

"You must be Alejandro," Maria said. "It is such a pleasure to meet you. I'm sure you are exhausted, though, so we can catch up later. Grace, will you please show Alejandro to his room. We have some pajamas waiting, along with a sandwich and some milk and cookies. You must be starved from your long journey. We thought you two," she nodded at Grace, "Could have a picnic in your room while we adults eat out here and discuss boring things."

Once again, Gabriella watched her mother in awe. Such a gracious woman.

Grace's cheeks pinked a little at the mention of her name, but she was over at Alejandro's side in an instant.

"My name is Grace," she said in perfect Italian. "Do you like to play Minecraft?"

The boy nodded enthusiastically as if someone was finally speaking his language in more ways than one. The two left the room deep in conversation.

#

Later, after all the adults had feasted on pasta Carbonara and fresh bread and salad at the twelve-foot long black dining table. The Saint stood and waited behind Maria's chair, saying it was time to get Maria to bed. He had hired a full-time nurse to care for Maria and she was waiting in the doorway. He'd also hired a nanny, who would remain employed until Gabriella and Donovan figured out their next steps.

When everyone had left the room and Gabriella and Donovan were alone, they didn't speak.

Gabriella stared at her plate, pushing around the last of her lemon tart.

Donovan was studiously ignoring Gabriella. Two could play at that game.

Grace appeared in the doorway. "Are you guys going to tuck me in and say prayers?"

When they were both home at night, bedtime duties were something they did as a team. But not tonight. Gabriella stood up, holding her plate.

"Grace, why don't you let Daddy tuck you in and I'll be in later for prayers. I just want to get some of this cleaned up first."

Her daughter wasn't falling for it. Staring down at her feet, she left the room without looking at either one of them.

Donovan and Gabriella exchanged a glance, a look between parents that said more than words ever could. Then Donovan turned away and the moment was gone. That familiar moment as parents was comforting and heartbreaking at the same time.

He got up to go tuck Grace in and Gabriella did the dishes.

Later, when Gabriella fell into bed, exhausted, Donovan wasn't there.

In the morning she found he'd fallen asleep on the couch in the family room watching TV. He made a joke of it to Grace, but when it began happening every night that week, it was clear it was no accident.

For the rest of the week, he kept her at a distance. Whenever she caught his eye, the pain on his face broke her heart. She was hurting too, though. It wasn't all about him. But it seemed like every chance they had to speak, Grace was there, holding his hand, clinging to him so she would never lose him again.

Donovan spent most of his days waking late and then working until past dinner at the DEA office, going through "debriefings" he said. They planned to bring Gabriella in the following week for her own interview.

So far, Gabriella had avoided contacting her newspaper. She'd sent a text to Kellogg saying she'd write the story about her abduction and *El Loro* for the newspaper and would be in touch within the next few weeks. But she didn't want to talk to him on the phone and ignored all calls and emails. She had lied. She wasn't writing anything.

She wasn't ready to talk to anyone except her immediate family. Her friends and colleagues seemed like part of a past life, a world she no longer lived in. Her brothers and sisters-in-law kept calling and she said she'd see them Sunday at Nana's. Her grandmother now had a live-in nurse, like her mother, but still hosted the Big Sunday Dinner every week.

On nearly every Sunday of her childhood, Gabriella had joined her large extended family at her grandmother's stone cottage out in Livermore. The house was tucked back among rolling hills covered with grapevines. On Sundays cars double and triple parked in front of the house and down the driveway for at least a quarter of a mile. Her grandmother was getting up there in years and a few years back, her grandchildren had taken over the meatball and sauce duties. Nowadays, Nana sat back and relaxed in her favorite chair on Sundays observing her legacy as people talked, laughed and ate. It was one of Gabriella's most cherished family traditions and she was especially happy to see that it had become important to Grace, as well.

She wondered what Alejandro would think about it.

He was a quiet boy.

Gabriella had received special permission to care for the boy until the international red tape had been sorted out. Nobody could find any living relatives in Italy.

The second day he was home, Alejandro had been evaluated by a therapist who said the boy was still in shock from being kidnapped and held captive for so long only to be freed and find out his father was murdered. The good news was that from what the therapist could tell, he had been treated well during his imprisonment. The therapist's recommendation to the government officials who had hired him was that the boy should not be uprooted again. At least not for a long while.

That was just fine by Gabriella.

Every day that first week she asked Alejandro if everything was okay, if he needed anything, if there was anything she could do?

He always shook his head no. He never asked for anything. But he followed Gabriella around. If she went into the living room, he'd bring his books there to study. If she went to her bedroom, he'd pack up and retreat to his own room. It was sweet, but heartbreaking at the same time.

A tutor was hired to teach him English at the penthouse. All paid for by The Saint, who seemed to have a soft spot for the boy.

One day, after they had been back about a week, Gabriella woke early, made a few phone calls. Once Grace was off to school, Gabriella headed to the family room.

Donovan had taken to staying up late and sleeping most of the morning. The living room, which could be closed off with glass doors, smelled like beer and funk.

She slammed open the glass door so hard, it crashed into the wall with a loud bang. Donovan woke with a scowl. She stood there shaking with anger.

"We're going to counseling. We have an appointment at ten."

Donovan watched her with bleary eyes. "Okay."

She turned and left without answering.

CHAPTER FIFTY-THREE

Donovan reached for Gabriella's hand as they walked into the office building where the therapist's office was located. That small gesture filled her with hope and gratefulness.

Maybe they could get past this.

Inside, the therapist's office was set up like a small living room with a series of plush chairs in a circle facing one another. The therapist, a small woman in a dark purple suit, stuck out her hand. "I'm Jeannine," she said.

After introductions, she asked what brought them to see her.

For a brief moment, Gabriella and Donovan looked at each other and laughed. Jeannine smiled, probably thinking this was going to an easy day of marital counseling. Donovan held his arm out to Gabriella. "Why don't you start? You're the storyteller."

Gabriella nodded. She could sum up the hell her life had been for the past five months.

When she was done, the therapist looked stunned and scooted back in her chair. She'd been leaning intently forward listening, taking notes and nodding. She let out a big whoosh of air and then turned to Donovan. "Anything you'd like to add?"

He shrugged and shook his head. "Nope. That about covers it."

The therapist opened her mouth to say something then closed it again.

The room was a silent for a moment, the only sound a passing airplane and traffic outside filtering in the cracked window.

As a reporter, Gabriella was trained to sit out any length of silence and let the other person fill in the awkward moment. As a detective, Donovan was even better at it.

After a long sixty seconds, the therapist stood. "I think that's enough for today. I will study my notes and we can resume on Thursday if that works for you." She held the door.

After the door closed behind them and they were heading to separate cars, Donovan turned to Gabriella. "She doesn't want to touch us with a ten-foot-pole."

Gabriella shook her head. "You're wrong. I think she's already trying to figure out how to write a book about our story."

Donovan burst into laughter.

But then he quickly sobered. Every time it seemed like they were resuming normal loving interactions, the memory of what happened in the jungle took over.

Opening her car door, Gabriella paused, watching as her husband looked down at the ground, swallowing. She waited for him to look back up at her. When he did, she spoke so softly she could barely hear her own words.

"I love you, Sean Donovan. I always will love you. No matter what."

He pressed his lips together, nodded, and turned away. She watched him get into his car. He was facing away, but she saw him raise a hand to his face and swipe it. Was he crying?

Gabriella slammed her car door and waited a second before turning the key over in the ignition. She'd done what she could. It was out of her hands now. If he wouldn't forgive her, that was his decision. She'd be heartbroken, but she'd survive. She was a Giovanni.

CHAPTER FIFTY-FOUR

That night Donovan came to her.

At first, she thought she was dreaming—feeling his mouth on her body—and by the time she was fully awake she was delirious with desire.

The way he felt. The way he smelled. The way he tasted.

Nobody would ever compare to Sean Donovan. Nobody could ever touch her like he did.

There was something about making love to a man that had spent years essentially memorizing and studying her body and how it reacted to his touch. There would never be anyone else who knew her so well, who knew how to arouse her.

In the black of night she couldn't see his face, but she felt the wetness on his cheeks. He was weeping as they made love. She burst into tears. He leaned down and whispered in her ear. "I love you forever. No matter what."

Her heart filled with joy. It was going to be okay.

After, she wept as he slept beside her. She cried in relief and in joy that she finally felt like she had her husband back. The stranger who had flown back from Central America with her was gone. Donovan was finally home.

But the next morning when she woke, she rolled over reaching for her husband. His spot in the bed was empty. She half sat up with bleary eyes. Donovan was sitting up in bed with his back to her, hands on his knees, head hanging down.

He spoke without looking at her.

"I rented an apartment nearby. At least for now—until we figure this out. It's a six-month lease."

She waited until he left the room before she rolled back over, burying her face in the pillow.

CHAPTER FIFTY-FIVE

Donovan and Gabriella saw each other at least twice a week—at their counseling sessions. In front of the counselor, they were guarded, words carefully chosen, emotions held in check. Both agreed that neither of them was ready to throw away their marriage, but neither was ready to pretend it was like it used to be, either.

Every once in a while, they would cross paths when Donovan came to get Grace and take her out for lunches and dinners and movies.

Gabriella never objected and was never jealous of their time together. They had a lot of time to make up as father and daughter.

Even with her parents living apart, it was the happiest Grace had been in months. Gabriella hadn't seen her daughter like that since before Donovan's plane crashed.

Each Tuesday and Thursday morning—the day of the marital counseling appointments—Gabriella dressed carefully, eyeing her closet for something she knew Donovan would like. She meticulously lined her eyes with black eyeliner, slicked on the petal pink lipstick her husband had always liked and spritzed on the perfume he had bought her every Christmas for the past decade.

She felt ridiculous and ashamed that she was trying to seduce her husband, but that, is in fact what she was doing. She knew that none of her superficial efforts mattered one bit, but still found she had to arm herself in this way before every counseling session.

Today, she was rewarded with an appreciated glance from Donovan when she walked in.

He stood and kissed her cheek. "You are beautiful."

Those three words nearly brought her to her knees. She fought back her tears. He must still love her, right? He had said he would love her forever, *no matter what*. But she also knew appreciating the way someone looked and loving someone had nothing to do with staying together. Nothing. Still, she clung to the way his voice sounded as he said it.

The tone of his voice, his glance, the kiss on the cheek. Baby steps. She'd take it.

Because it was only a few minutes later that the rage surfaced.

"I can't sleep," Donovan told the counselor. "All I think about … all I can see are those pictures."

At first, Gabriella had been sickened by comments like this, but now, three weeks into counseling, it was getting old.

Get. Over. It.

And that's where her rage flared.

"How do you feel thinking about those pictures?" the counselor prodded.

"Furious. Like I could kill someone." Donovan's neck grew red.

Gabriella's eyes widened. This was new. It sent a trickle of fear through her. She'd covered enough domestic violence stories in her career as a reporter to see how jealousy could make someone homicidal even to the love of their lives. It was an old story. It was common. But she'd never dreamed her own husband could feel this way.

"Who do you feel like you could kill?" The counselor was very careful in how she asked this. Gabriella had seen enough therapists over the years to know the counselor was holding her breath, wondering if this was one of those few comments that therapists were required to report to law enforcement. Everything said to a therapist was protected under the law—except a threat to someone else.

"That's the bitch about it," Donovan said with a bitter laugh. "There is nobody. Nobody who is still alive that is. Everyone I wish dead in this situation is already dead. Except me."

The therapist sat up straighter.

"Are you thinking about harming yourself?"

Fear raced through Gabriella. She'd never even considered that possibility.

But Donovan burst into laughter. "Hell no."

Relief filled Gabriella. And then anger.

"It looks like you have something you want to say to that, Gabriella?"

"I don't understand that desire—to wish someone dead." It was a total lie. She'd wished plenty of people dead—the man who kidnapped and killed her sister. The man who kidnapped and killed her niece. The man who kidnapped her. And here's the thing, this therapist had no clue, but Gabriella had killed all three of them.

She gave a strangled laugh as she realized this. That was for another counselor or another life. This woman didn't need to know any of this. But to her surprise, she found Donovan laughing loudly again. Not in a bitter way, but in a conspiratorial way with her. He knew her so well. He knew exactly what she was thinking.

"Well, this is progress,' the counselor said, brightly, clapping as she stood. "Let's stop for today and I'll see you both Thursday."

Donovan strode out of the office without saying goodbye, so Gabriella took her time gathering her things and then stopped at the office building's bathroom so she didn't have to run into Donovan in the parking lot. Her anger toward him was growing. He needed to get his shit together and make this marriage work.

The therapist had said it was normal to feel this rage toward one another, but it was also important to express it and then let it go. Today, she'd failed that directive. Both of them had. She was furious at him and he was furious at her.

However, she had to admit that after three weeks of counseling, some of the anger toward each other had dissipated. Enough so that Donovan sometimes called just to see how Gabriella was doing, even when Grace was at school.

As she drove home Donovan called.

"Hello?" Was he going to yell at her now that the counselor wasn't around?

"I was thinking," he paused. He sounded nervous. "We haven't made it out to Nana's yet for Sunday dinner. How about I come get you and Grace about ten on Sunday and we drive together?"

"Okay," Gabriella said in a small voice.

"Okay then." He hung up.

Nobody, not even Gabriella's mother, knew about their marital woes. Everybody in the family thought that they were still recovering from their ordeal and that's why they hadn't made Sunday dinners at grandmas yet.

They'd been able to keep it from Maria who had returned back to her Marin County home with her nurse the day after Gabriella and Donovan arrived home.

Maria had good days and bad and the last thing Gabriella wanted was for her mother to worry about her daughter's marriage.

Gabriella tried to stop by the house at least once every day to spend time with her mother. The doctors had said she could live another six months or go any day. Each morning Gabriella woke up with trepidation and before she had barely opened her eyes, would lean over to check her phone for messages from The Saint. Every morning the screen was blank, she gave thanks for another day with her mother.

On Sunday, Gabriella woke filled with hope and excitement. She loved Sunday dinner at Nana's. Today, she planned to spend lots of time with her mother. She also needed Maria's moral support because today was the day everyone in the Giovanni family would meet Alejandro. All they knew was that Gabriella and Donovan had taken in the orphan son of a colleague killed in Central America. And that was all they needed to know.

Gabriella had woken extra early to make a large dish of lasagna and bake a triple batch of biscotti to bring to the get together. Donovan offered to drive her old Saab so she could hold the lasagna on her lap in its insulated pan.

Grace was ecstatic in the back seat, talking nonstop to Alejandro about what it was like at her Nana's house.

"I think Carlos and Marcella are going to bring their iPads, too, so we can play Minecraft."

Donovan and Gabriella exchanged a look and without discussing it, came to an agreement. "No iPads," Donovan said lightly. "You're going to leave yours in the car. This is a chance to spend time with your family. You and your cousins can play outside."

"You are so mean!" Grace burst out.

"You better watch it or you'll lose your electronic privileges for the week." "Don't worry," Gabriella said. "Your cousins might think they are going to play on their iPads while they're at Nana's, but they are wrong."

Grace rolled her eyes, but Gabriella pretended she didn't see it.

It all seemed so normal. Like a normal family having a morning spat. Looking in the mirror, Gabriella saw Grace cross her arms angrily. Alejandro was looking out the window.

Not for the first time, she wondered if she was doing the right thing in taking the boy in to her home.

But it felt right. A feeling of contentment settled on Gabriella. The long driveway to her grandmother's house always filled Gabriella with peace. It was no different today. Right then, at that moment, all was okay in her world. And it would have to be enough.

She rolled down her window and let the breeze whip her hair, inhaling the country smells. For the first time since she'd come home, she let go of all her worries and fears.

CHAPTER FIFTY-SIX

Gabriella opened her eyes to see several faces staring down at her with concern. The last thing she remembered was being in her grandmother's backyard, kneeling at her mother's side, and then standing. Now she was flat on her back on the grass.

"What happened?"

"You fainted? How do you feel?" It was Donovan with such a concerned look in his eyes she wanted to cry. He did still love her.

"I feel okay. I don't remember what happened."

"You started to stand and then tipped. Donovan caught you before you hit the ground," it was her sister-in-law Nina. "Do you want a drink?"

Gabriella nodded and tried to sit up, but it triggered a wave of nausea. "Oh God, I feel sick. I better not drink anything."

She glanced around the big backyard. Thank God not very many people had noticed her fainting. More than a dozen kids still raced through the backyard garden under grape vines strung from trellises and through waist-high tomato and pepper plants. A large tree toward the back of the lot shaded a small alcove with a wrought iron table and chairs where some of the older uncles sat smoking cigars, banished from the main patio by her grandmother.

On the large patio, flowered tablecloths covered half a dozen tables already spread with wine, water carafes, baskets of bread and appetizers. Gabriella took it all in with relief. The scene was as familiar to her as her own face in the mirror.

Donovan lifted her by her armpits and sat her in a chair by her mother. Maria was watching carefully. "Mom, I swear I'm okay. I promise."

"Go to the doctor. Tomorrow. Do you understand?" Maria's voice was sharp.

"Yes, mama."

"You promise?"

"Yes, I promise."

Donovan laughed. "Well, that was easy. I've been telling her to go get checked out all week. I should have just called Mama Maria. She gets the job done."

Gabriella could see that Donovan's laughter hid his worry. He was working the muscle in his jaw something fierce. And he'd only asked her yesterday to go get checked out when she threw up while they were on the phone. He'd been telling her all week? Whatever.

It was uncomfortable having everyone staring at her, so Gabriella was relieved when her other sisters-in-laws and nieces brought out dishes of food and put them on the long wooden tables under the grape arbor nearby.

Nana hobbled out with her cane and pursed her lips in her earsplitting whistle. It was nearly unbelievable that such a shrieking sound could come out of a four foot five inch, ninety-pound woman.

At her whistle, all the kids gathered with the adults on the patio. Gabriella's brother, Marco, said a prayer before everyone scrambled to get a spot at the table. The children, who outnumbered the adults the past few years, would sit at a series of small round metal tables nearby after they filled their plates from the main table.

Platters of pork chops, Italian sausages and spaghetti were placed on the large table alongside heaping piles of meatballs, baskets of bread, and bowls of green salad. In addition, several plates of vegetables were passed, along with a dozen carafes of water or wine.

Gabriella picked at her food. She was ravenous, but afraid if she ate too much or too quickly, she'd get sick. She'd concentrate on the meatballs. She'd been anemic in the past, so maybe her body needed some iron and that's why she'd fainted. She caught her mother giving her a concerned glance. Ridiculous to pass out and worry her mother who already had so much to think about.

She'd go to the doctor in the morning and then reassure her mother that nothing was wrong. But just in case she wasn't right, she was planning to lie and tell them she couldn't get into the doctor until Tuesday. That way if something weren't okay, she'd have a day to figure out how to tell her mother. Because despite her seeming nonchalance, something didn't feel right in her body.

CHAPTER FIFTY-SEVEN

"I'm pregnant."

Gabriella stumbled on the two simple words, knowing deep in her heart that they were the death knell for her marriage.

She had asked Donovan to dinner and as soon as Grace had gone to bed, led him out to the penthouse deck near the pool with two glasses and a bottle of Bourbon, hoping the alcohol, along with the beauty of the velvet night sky and stars would ease the shock of her words. But of course they couldn't.

As if emotions had physical form, the atmosphere on the penthouse roof turned dark and ugly as soon as she spoke.

Without answering, Donovan reached over and poured a giant swig of Bourbon, downed it, and poured another. Any ground they had gained through counseling was gone.

"I wanted to tell you as soon as possible," Gabriella said. "I took the test this afternoon at the doctor's office. That's why I was rushing Grace to bed tonight, so we could be alone and talk."

"She's got a right to know, too," Donovan said in a dead voice Gabriella didn't recognize. "She's got a little half brother or sister coming now."

"That's not fair. You don't know that," Gabriella said, but she did know. If you thought about it, did the math, it was more likely it was Nico's than Donovan's.

As if reading her mind, Donovan asked, "How far along are you?"

"I don't know."

"You're having it for sure?"

"I wanted to talk to you about it."

"It's not really my decision, is it?"

"You're my husband. We are a family. I want to talk to you about it."

"I've got nothing to say," he said. He leaned over and poured another large glass of bourbon, downing that as quickly as the first. Then he stood abruptly, setting the glass down sideways so it tipped over, nearly rolling of the table onto the cement. Gabriella lunged for the glass, catching it in time. When she looked up, Donovan had already disappeared inside the penthouse.

Staring at the stars peeking through the drifting clouds, Gabriella tried to calm herself and push down the bitter disappointment she felt over Donovan's reaction. She knew he wouldn't be overjoyed, but she thought he would understand. She thought he would still stand by her and they could rebuild their family. But it might be too late.

When she finally composed herself enough to go inside, Donovan was gone.

#

The next day, he wouldn't answer her calls. The following night, he didn't show up when he was supposed to take Grace out to dinner. Gabriella made an excuse for him. She told their daughter he had called earlier and said he was sick.

"Why did you let me get dressed and wait until the last minute to tell me," Grace shouted, face red, fists clenched at her side.

"I'm so sorry, honey. I forgot." Gabriella looked away as she said it.

"You're a mean mother. You only care about yourself." Grace stomped into the other room.

Gabriella looked over at Alejandro who was sitting at the kitchen table doing English homework. "*Mi dispiace*," she said. I'm sorry. Gabriella was taking a refresher course in Italian so she could help the boy feel more comfortable even as he learned English.

CHAPTER FIFTY-EIGHT

Donovan eyed his service weapon. It would be quick and painless.

He didn't think he could stand the pain anymore. It was more than he could take.

Gabriella would be better off without him. He didn't deserve her. And how could he face his daughter when she grew old enough to hear and realize what he had done – how he had not only slept with another woman, but fallen in love with her.

Because that is what hurt the most. He loved Monica. But he also loved Gabriella. It was ripping him apart.

And worse. He had done what he vowed to never ever do: He had become an adulterer. Just like his father, that son-of-bitch.

He had done to his wife what his father had done to his mother. He was no better than that loser who had turned his sweet mother into an angry bitter woman.

CHAPTER FIFTY-NINE

Four days after Donovan stomped out, he didn't show up for the counseling appointment.

"Do we need to worry?" The therapist asked.

"No. I'll make sure he's at Thursday's appointment," Gabriella said and left. She knew why the therapist had asked that. It was that crack Donovan made a few weeks ago during therapy:

Everyone I wish dead in this situation is already dead. Except me.

She fought off her increasing dread during the drive to Donovan's apartment. Once there, she knocked and rang the doorbell for ten minutes. Nothing. She took out her lock pick set and popped open his door.

From the smell that whooshed out of the room—sour sweat and alcohol and mustiness—it was clear he'd been here the whole time. The empty booze bottles scattered everywhere told the story.

He'd been on a bender.

Making her way through the messy apartment, she headed to the bedroom. He was naked in bed. At first, when she couldn't see his chest rising and falling in sleep, her heart skipped into her throat, panic overcoming her in an ice-cold chill.

Then he moaned in his sleep.

Thank God.

Leaning over him, she gently smoothed the hair back from his face. He gave a small sound of contentment, but stayed asleep.

Despite herself, she kissed his forehead lightly and then drew back, pulling a wadded-up blanket over most of his body. Several empty water bottles were on the nightstand. At least he knew enough in his drunken stupor to stay hydrated. She threw away the empty bottles and left three large glasses of water in their place on the nightstand. Gabriella left a note under one glass of water on the nightstand asking Donovan to please call Grace because their daughter was worried about him.

The apartment was a disaster.

Pieces of broken furniture, torn clothing and shredded paintings littered the floors and every available surface. He had been in a destructive rage. The flat screen TV was smashed into shards.

Several slips of paper on the counter showed he'd been having bottles of whiskey and sub sandwiches delivered from a local store. The last one was dated the day before.

Gabriella was tempted to start cleaning his apartment, but realized that was enabling his fucked-up behavior. So instead, she slipped out of the apartment, locking the door behind her.

During her appointment earlier that day, the one that Donovan had missed, the therapist had said Donovan couldn't accept the fact that she was pregnant. Because to him, a baby was living forever proof of Gabriella's infidelity. Although Donovan had finally accepted that when Gabriella slept with Nico because she truly believed she was a widow, he couldn't accept that that union had resulted in a baby.

Well, tough shit. It was time for him to grow up and get over it.

Gabriella slammed the front door as she left.

#

That night the phone rang and Grace answered it. "Daddy!"

Grace paced with the phone smiling at Gabriella, talking excitedly about her day. Gabriella hovered nearby in case Grace seemed upset by something Donovan said, but it all seemed to be fine.

After ten minutes, Grace pushed the end button and skipped off into her room.

Donovan never asked to speak to Gabriella and she never reached for the phone.

Two days later, Donovan showed up at their next counseling appointment. He never mentioned missing the previous appointment, nor his bender.

When the therapist tried to bring up Gabriella's pregnancy, Donovan stood up and headed for the door. "I'm not ready to talk about that."

The therapist conceded, putting up her palm. "Sit back down. We'll hold off on that for now."

"This is bullshit," Gabriella said, standing up. "He doesn't have to deal with any of this? Is that what you're saying? He gets a free pass?"

The therapist swallowed and started to talk, but Gabriella continued.

"Guess what? I'd like a "get out of jail free," or "go directly to go and collect two hundred dollars' card," too. But I obviously have to fucking deal with it. I can't just check out and drink myself into oblivion. I have to be an adult and deal with it. When I married you," now she turned to Donovan. "It was for better or for worse. Well, guess what? This is the 'for worse,' part. You are chastising me for breaking my marriage vows, when you did the same damn thing. You are a hypocrite. I've forgiven you. But I'm telling you now—you have one more chance to live up to your marriage vows, Sean Donovan. This is it. If you can't handle this—this baby—then we might as well just stop coming here altogether because I'm fucking done apologizing. The ball is in your court."

She stalked out, slamming the door behind her as hard as she could.

Sitting alone in the gynecologist's office, Gabriella steeled herself for the exam ahead. With Grace, Donovan had been there for every pre-natal visit. He'd held her hand during a tense moment when they couldn't find a heartbeat right away. He'd been there during the first ultrasound where they could see Grace's profile in 3D and watch her sucking her thumb in the womb.

But for this pregnancy, she was on her own.

Gabriella grew angry thinking about it. So much for through thickness and thin.

The wind howled outside the window and dark clouds made the day seem even more ominous. Rain began to splat on the window loudly. It was a shitty day and she was in a shitty mood.

She placed her palms flat on her stomach. Even though the baby was too young to kick and be felt, she wanted some reassurance that it was still healthy and alive inside her.

She'd had miscarriages before. She knew she wouldn't be able to relax until she was further along.

That hadn't been her first reaction upon learning she was pregnant this time around. Her first reaction was to get rid of the baby.

But she also knew she couldn't live with that decision. Now, she didn't even want to admit that losing this baby was a possibility.

She wanted this baby and wanted it badly. And she knew she would sacrifice the life she had now for it. Because that is what she was doing by choosing to have the baby. Because having this baby meant her marriage was over. It would ruin any chance she and Donovan had to save their relationship. But it wasn't her fault. It was his choice. He was making the decision.

Already, Grace was getting used to living with parents who kept separate homes and even said yesterday she was looking forward to a little brother or sister. She loved having Alejandro around and once in a fit of anger told Gabriella she had been selfish for making Grace an only child.

This morning she talked excitedly about getting to decorate her new room at Donovan's place. With so many of her classmate's parents divorced, it wasn't that big of a deal to her. Or at least that's how she was acting.

Any way that Gabriella looked at it, choosing to keep this baby marked the beginning of the end. Donovan would never accept this baby as his own. He could barely accept that she had sex with another man. Which was total bullshit. He hadn't had any problem fucking another woman over and over in that basement below her. They both had made mistakes.

The worst part was that her heart ached for Donovan every single day. More than anything she wanted the life she used to have. Before everything went to hell.

But it wasn't the same and wouldn't ever be the same again.

She got her husband back only to lose him again.

Now, on this dark dreary day, she would be able to see the baby inside her for the first time. Once she looked at that little curled shrimp-like body on the ultrasound, that baby was hers forever.

Looking around the waiting room, Gabriella realized she was the oldest mother there. The other pregnant women looked to be in their twenties. That's okay. She could handle it. So what if she were a little more tired than she'd been with Grace. She'd probably also be a little more patient, right?

The petite nurse in the Hello Kitty scrubs opened the door from the inner offices. Everyone in the waiting room looked up expectantly as she consulted the clipboard she was holding. "Gabriella Giovanni?" The nurse looked around the room with a smile until Gabriella gave a small wave and stood, smoothing her skirt down.

She was nearly to the nurse when the outer door slammed open, letting in a whoosh of rainstorm-scented cold air along with a long eerie howling sound from the wind. Everyone turned to look.

It was Donovan. He stood panting, his hair wet and sticking up from the rain and wind. The front of his shirt soaked.

Gabriella met his eyes.

"I'm here," he said.

ENOVELLAS,
AND EXCLUSIVE GABRIELLA GIOVANNI MATERIAL

My readers mean everything to me. To keep in touch, I send monthly (okay sometimes they arrive every *other* month) newsletters with details on special offers, contests and new releases.

And if you sign up for the newsletter, I'll send you all this free stuff:

1. Death Under the Stone Arch Bridge. The first in a series of three novellas featuring photojournalist Tommy St. James.
2. The Saint. A Gabriella Giovanni enovella that is a prequel to the award-nominated mystery series.
3. The Gabriella Giovanni Cookbook
4. CIA Dossier on Gabriella Giovanni

You can get the novel, the novellas, and the exclusive material, **for free**, by signing up here: http://eepurl.com/chwVkT
Or here: http://www.kristibelcamino.com/contact/newsletter/

DID YOU LIKE THIS BOOK?

Reviews are the lifeblood of this author business. Reviews, honest reviews, mean the world to me. They don't have to be fancy, either. Nobody is critiquing you on your review. And they don't always have to be five-star, either. What matters is that people are reading and have opinions on my books. I am a fairly new writer and don't have the marketing push that many other writers do that gets their books out in front of other readers.

What I do have is you.

I am unbelievably lucky to have very passionate and loyal readers who take the time to let me know what they think of my books (and sometimes even where they think I could improve).

If you liked this book, I would be extremely grateful if you could take a few minutes out of your day to leave a review on Amazon. As I said, it doesn't need to be long or involved, anything will help. Thank you!

GIA IN THE CITY OF THE DEAD
Coming October 2017

When Gia Valentina Santella's parents died four years ago, she fled small town Monterey to pursue the high life in the big city where she could smother her grief by playing house in a luxurious high-rise apartment with sweeping views of the Golden Gate Bridge.

Armed with a hefty inheritance, it didn't take long for Gia to carve out an empty life for herself in San Francisco, slumming at art school, racing her red Ferrari up and down the coast, and getting hammered at the city's finest establishments.

Then one day, a letter comes in the mail and everything changes. The death of Gia's parents was no accident. They were murdered.

Now, Gia must find who really killed her parents at the same time she's frantically trying to keep one step ahead of the murderer who is now intent on making her his next victim.

COMING OCTOBER 2017. Read on for exclusive excerpt.

EXCLUSIVE EXCERPT

Coming soon …
GIA in the City of the Dead

By Kristi Belcamino

North Beach, San Francisco

I eyed the brunette in the sparkly underwear as she whipped her long hair and draped her tanned legs around the silver pole, sliding one stiletto-heeled foot up and down, up and down.

Her breasts, naked and swinging, were bigger than mine, but she was about the same size and weight. No stretch marks on her stomach or breasts, hips still slim. Childless. No thin white band on her ring finger. Single. Fake diamond studs. Not doing this for fun or to rebel against daddy. Fuchsia toenail polish. Definitely *not* from the Bay Area. Perfect white teeth and flawless skin. Not a crankster. No identifying tattoos.

She would do.

I slid three twenties under the strap of her G-string and told her to meet me in the private room at her break.

Waiting in the tiny, mirrored room, I rummaged around in my bag for a roach, but came up empty. Must have smoked it last night. At the bottom of my purse, my fingers brushed some loose shake so I licked them and stuck them back into my bag. I poked around until tiny green flecks stuck to the pads of my fingers, which I licked again. I was plucking a few stray flakes off my lipstick when she walked in, wiping tiny beads of sweat away from her temple with a small white towel.

She leaned back against the door and untied her short silky robe.

"Hey, honey. What's your name?" she asked, fluffing her hair. My back was to her, but I didn't take my eyes off her face in the mirror.

"Gia," I said and smiled. Yes, she would do perfectly.

"I'm Desiree." *Sure you are*. She sidled up to me, pressing her bare breast against my arm from behind, trailing her fingers down my lips as we watched ourselves in the floor-length mirror.

"It's not what you think," I said, gently pushing her away.

Ten minutes later we had a deal.

I slipped back into the night, ignoring the groups of men huddled on the neon sidewalks outside, smoking and cat calling everyone who looked like they might have a vagina — whether they were born that way or not.

Chapter 1

The previous week

The throbbing head pain keeping time with my heartbeat told me last night had been a doozy. Even if I didn't remember any of it.

Without opening my eyes, I knew it was time to get up because I could hear the noisy gurgling of my Nespresso in the kitchen. The espresso machine was programmed to kick on at two every afternoon so when I rolled out of bed, hot coffee would be waiting. It was a rough life.

I stretched and yawned and then froze at the sound of clanging in my kitchen. I rummaged around under my huge stack of pillows for my gun and then a vague memory returned — I'd brought some guy home from the bar last night. I groaned. He should've been long gone. I put the gun back. If he was banging pots and pans around in the kitchen, he probably wasn't a rapist or serial killer.

I yanked the covers up over my naked breasts when a curly haired head peeked around the doorframe. "Hey, Gia. You hungry? It'll be ready in a jiffy."

I stared until his head withdrew. He whistled as he walked back to the kitchen. That did it. This guy was way too chipper to be my type. I closed my eyes trying to piece together what had happened the night before. I vaguely remembered the bartender at Anarchy refusing to fill my glass again. How much had I had to drink? It must have been a lot because Scott had never cut me off before. The last thing I remembered was stomping off looking for someone else at the bar to order my tequila for me and some cute, curly-haired guy had smiled at me.

He seemed harmless. I shrugged on my kimono and tried to avoid looking into the mirrored doors on my closet as I walked past, but still managed to get a glimpse of a green silk robe wearing Broom Hilda with wild hair. I stopped in the bathroom to splash some water on my face, again avoiding the mirror. Relief washed over me when I spotted a neatly tied up condom in the metal trashcan. Time to face my houseguest.

I leaned on the doorframe into the small kitchen. The guy was putting slices of sourdough bread in my toaster. Eggs and milk were on the counter. Butter was sizzling in a frying pan on the stove. The guy *was* cute. But none of that mattered. I cleared my throat. He looked up and smiled.

"Listen …" I closed my eyes for a second. "I'm sure you're really sweet. But you have to leave now."

When I opened my eyes, his smile faded.

I tried again. "I drank a lot last night. I don't remember much but I do know that I probably did some things I shouldn't have and it's better if you leave. Now."

"Hey, I'm a feminist," he said, holding his palms out. "I don't take advantage of drunk women. If anything, you talked me into it. I kept saying it probably wasn't a good idea, but you insisted otherwise. You practically dragged me back here."

I cringed. He was probably right. But I still needed to get rid of this nameless, chivalrous stranger.

"Like I said," I began. "You seem like a really nice guy. But you need to go."

"No problem." He didn't seem angry, only disappointed, which sent a stab of guilt through me. But I needed this stranger out of my house immediately.

He grabbed a leather jacket off my dining room table. I noticed an empty wine bottle and two glasses on the table along with what looked like the remains of a pumpkin pie. Guess I had brought the party back here.

When I finally heard the door click closed, I sunk onto the chair on my balcony with a cup of espresso and a pack of Dunhills. I felt another stab of guilt remembering the guy's face when I told him to leave. I consoled myself with the thought that he was too nice and therefore too good for me, anyway. I'd actually probably done him a favor by booting him out before he started to really like me.

I spent at least an hour sitting on my balcony, feet up on the rail in my fuzzy slippers, watching the fog burn off the bay until the Golden Gate Bridge came into view and beyond that the Marin headlands. If I looked over my shoulder, I could see the new span of the Bay Bridge stretching across the Bay, gleaming in the sunlight.

It looked like a good day to take my Ferrari out on the open road. It was one of those days where I needed to drive as fast as I could for as long as I could. Having a stranger sleep in my bed with me only made me feel lonelier than ever.

Acknowledgments

I would not have had the confidence to put this book out without the keen insight and feedback from several people, including Sarah Hanley, Sharon Long, John Bychowski, Erin Alford, Liz Cronk, Doug Cronk, Emily Goehner, Taloo Carrillo, Mimi Ryan and Anissa Kennedy! Thank you!

ABOUT THE AUTHOR:

Kristi Belcamino is a Macavity, Barry, and Anthony Award-nominated author, a newspaper cops reporter, and an Italian mama who makes a tasty biscotti. As an award-winning crime reporter at newspapers in California, she flew over Big Sur in an FA-18 jet with the Blue Angels, raced a Dodge Viper at Laguna Seca and watched autopsies.

Her books feature strong, fierce, and independent women facing unspeakable evil in order to seek justice for those unable to do so themselves.

Belcamino has written and reported about many high-profile cases including the Laci Peterson murder and Chandra Levy's disappearance. She has appeared on Inside Edition and her work has appeared in the New York Times, Writer's Digest, Miami Herald, San Jose Mercury News, and Chicago Tribune. Kristi now works part-time as a police reporter at the St. Paul Pioneer Press. She lives in Minneapolis with her husband and her two fierce daughters.

Find out more at http://www.kristibelcamino.com. Find her on Facebook at https://www.facebook.com/kristibelcaminowriter/ or on Twitter @KristiBelcamino. Sign up for her newsletter here http://www.kristibelcamino.com/contact/newsletter/

ALSO BY KRISTI BELCAMINO

The Gabriella Giovanni Series

BLESSED ARE THE DEAD

Nominated for a Macavity Award for Best First Mystery Novel and an Anthony Award for Best First Novel, BLESSED ARE THE DEAD, the first book in the Gabriella Giovanni Mystery Series, was inspired by Kristi Belcamino's dealings on the crime beat with a serial killer.

To catch a killer, one reporter must risk it all ...

San Francisco Bay Area newspaper reporter Gabriella Giovanni spends her days on the crime beat, flitting in and out of other people's nightmares, yet walking away unscathed. When a little girl disappears on the way to the school bus stop, her quest for justice and a front-page story leads her to a convicted kidnapper, Jack Dean Johnson, who reels her in with promises to reveal his exploits as a serial killer. But Gabriella's passion for her job quickly spirals into obsession when she begins to suspect the kidnapper may have ties to her own dark past: her sister's murder. Risking her life, her job, and everything she holds dear, Gabriella embarks on a quest to find answers and stop a deranged murderer before he strikes again. Perfect for fans of Sue Grafton and Laura Lippman's Tess Monaghan series!

BUY HERE: https://www.amazon.com/Blessed-are-Dead-Gabriella-Mysteries/dp/0062338919/

BLESSED ARE THE MEEK

A rash of high-profile murders all point to Giovanni's boyfriend, Detective Sean Donovan, when investigators uncover a single link in the deaths: Annalisa Cruz. A decade ago, Cruz seduced Donovan away from a life as a monk, and though their relationship soured long ago ... her passion for him has not.
As the investigation continues, it becomes increasingly clear that any man who gets involved with Cruz soon ends up dead, including a dot-com millionaire, the mayor of San Francisco, and a police officer. Donovan, the only man to have dated Cruz and survived, is arrested for the murders and dubbed a jealous ex, leaving Gabriella

scrambling to find the real killer without ending up as the next body headed for the morgue.

Gabriella's search ultimately unearths a dark secret that Donovan had intended to take to the grave. Faced with the knowledge of this terrible truth, Gabriella must tie the past and present together to clear Donovan's name.

BUY HERE: https://www.amazon.com/Blessed-are-Meek-Gabriella-Mysteries/dp/0062338935/

BLESSED ARE THOSE WHO WEEP

This **Amazon Bestselling Mystery by Kristi Belcamino is nominated for a 2016 Barry Award for Best Original Paperback** and has been called "a crackling, emotional, and rocket-paced mystery" by New York Times bestselling author Lisa Unger.

San Francisco Bay Area newspaper crime reporter Gabriella Giovanni stumbles onto a horrific crime scene with only one survivor--a baby girl found crawling between the dead bodies of her family members. Reeling from the slaughter, Gabriella clings to the infant. When Social Services pries the little girl from her arms, the enormity of the tragedy hits home. Diving deep into a case that brings her buried past to the forefront, Gabriella is determined to hunt down the killer who left this helpless baby an orphan.

But one by one the clues all lead to a dead end, and Gabriella's obsession with finding justice pulls her into a dark, tortuous spiral that is set to destroy everything she loves ...

BUY HERE: https://www.amazon.com/Blessed-are-Those-Who-Weep/dp/0062389394/

BLESSED ARE THOSE WHO MOURN

San Francisco Bay Area newspaper crime reporter Gabriella Giovanni has finally got it all together: a devoted and loving boyfriend, Detective Sean Donovan; a beautiful little girl with him; and her dream job as the cops' reporter for the *Bay Herald*. But her success has been hard-won and has left her with debilitating paranoia. When a string of young co-eds starts to show up dead with suspicious Biblical verses left on their bodies--the same verses that the man she suspects kidnapped and murdered her sister twenty years ago had sent to her--she begins to question if the killer is trying to send her a message.

It is not until evil strikes Gabriella's own family that her worst fears are confirmed. As the clock begins to tick, every passing hour means the difference between life and death to those Gabriella loves...

BUY HERE: https://www.amazon.com/Blessed-are-Those-Who-Mourn/dp/0062389416/

CITY OF ANGELS

Nikki Black, a self-imposed lone wolf since her mother died, fled suburban Chicago to escape her painful past. But when her so-called boyfriend reveals why he really lured her to Southern California, she ends up on the streets of L.A. with only the clothes on her back and a destitute twelve-year-old named Rain following in her shadows. The girls seek refuge at a residential hotel above a punk rock bar in downtown L.A. a few months before the city erupts into chaos during the 1992 riots. At The American Hotel, Nikki makes friends and, for the first time in years, feels as if she has a real family again. But everything changes when Rain disappears. Everyone believes Rain succumbed to the seductive allure of addiction and life on the streets. Determined to find Rain, Nikki burrows deeper into the underbelly of a city that hides a darkness beneath the glamour. And when she unveils a sinister cover-up by a powerful group that secretly controls the city of angels, she could lose everything, including her life. *City of Angels* is an edgy, gritty, mature Young Adult mystery about a young woman's struggle to not only belong — but survive.

BUY HERE: https://www.amazon.com/City-Angels-Kristi-Belcamino/dp/1943818436

LETTERS FROM A SERIAL KILLER

Letters from a Serial Killer is about two women and their quest to find Xiana Fairchild, who was snatched off the streets of Vallejo on her way to the school bus stop and never seen again.

It is about the mother who raised Xiana and the newspaper reporter who covered the story.

In this book, Kristi Belcamino and Stephanie Kahalekulu share details of their jailhouse conversations with the man who took Xiana, the letters he sent from behind bars and how they are forever bonded by their dealings with a monster, but more than that--by their quest for justice for Xiana.
"After termination ... there is a letdown. Anytime you get an adrenaline rush like that, there's a letdown. Hard enough where it puts you to sleep." - Curtis Dean Anderson from jail.

This novella is a blend of true crime and memoir about what happens when a child goes missing and gives eerie insight - through letters and jailhouse conversations - into the mind of a killer who preys on little girls.

BUY HERE: https://www.amazon.com/Letters-Serial-Killer-Kristi-Belcamino/dp/1523954906/

COPYRIGHT

All the characters in this book are fictitious and any resemblance to actual persons living or dead is entirely coincidental.

66446956R00192

Made in the USA
Lexington, KY
14 August 2017